CW01212103

Deadly Degrees in the Pyrenees

Deadly Degrees in the Pyrenees

Elly Grant

Copyright (C) 2017 Elly Grant
Layout design and Copyright (C) 2017 Creativia
Published 2017 by Creativia
Cover art by Art Evit
This book is a work of fiction. Names, characters, places, and incidents are the product of the author's imagination or are used fictitiously. Any resemblance to actual events, locales, or persons, living or dead, is purely coincidental.

All rights reserved. No part of this book may be reproduced or transmitted in any form or by any means, electronic or mechanical, including photocopying, recording, or by any information storage and retrieval system, without the author's permission.

For more information and to buy copies, you can link to Elly author page on Amazon at

http://www.amazon.com/Elly-Grant/e/B008DGF83W/

or http://www.amazon.co.uk/Elly-Grant/e/B008DGF83W/

or visit her website at http://ellygrant.wix.com/ellygrant

Books by the Author

Death in the Pyrenees series:

- Palm Trees in the Pyrenees
- Grass Grows in the Pyrenees
- Red Light in the Pyrenees
- Dead End in the Pyrenees
- Deadly Degrees in the Pyrenees

Angela Murphy series:

- The Unravelling of Thomas Malone
- The Coming of the Lord

Also by Elly Grant

- Never Ever Leave Me
- Death at Presley Park
- But Billy Can't Fly
- Twists and Turns

Chapter 1

When the woman first began to feel too hot, she tried to tough it out, convincing herself she could take it. Besides, the sauna was great for her skin, but after another few minutes she knew she'd had enough. Her face was flushed, her temperature raised and sweat was no longer forming in droplets on her skin. Definitely time to call it a day, she thought.

Pushing on the door, she was surprised to find it unyielding. Sauna doors are designed to withstand extreme changes in temperature. They do not warp. The woman put her shoulder to it. Still it didn't budge. Her stomach began to cramp and fear crept in. Why was the door stuck? How could it be stuck? She stared out of the tempered, safety-glass panel.

"Help, help!" she called, banging on the glass. "Is anybody there? Help, help me, I'm stuck in the sauna!" She paused, listening, but she heard no sounds, only silence.

Realising her plight, she began to panic and scream, long, keening animal-like sounds. Her temperature rose even higher. Painful spasms wracked her legs and hands. She became confused, throwing herself against the side walls of the sauna in an attempt to escape, then trying to kick her way out by pounding her bare heels on the wooden floor.

Eventually, she collapsed with exhaustion and heat stroke. She lost consciousness and fell into a coma before her body succumbed to shock.

Her corpse was discovered hours later, when her lover arrived for a romantic liaison. There was nothing romantic about what he found. The ghastly sight of the broiled woman with her red skin and bulging, bloodshot eyes would stay with him for the rest of his life.

Michelle Moliner's murderer had planned to kill her. This was not an accident, not a random act of burglary gone wrong. Her killer knew she'd be alone and vulnerable. Her killer wanted her to burn in hell.

* * *

It had been a beautiful morning. The sun was shining through a chink in the curtains. Michelle stretched lazily, spreading out her limbs in the comfortable, king-sized bed. Even though she and Jacques no longer shared a bedroom, she was pleased he had gone away with his club and she had the house to herself. Michelle planned to have a gloriously indulgent day. She had first stirred when Jacques banged about the house, getting ready for his weekend. He was a clumsy man and didn't make any effort to be quiet on her account. She heard the front door slam, the squeal of the hinges on the tall, electrically controlled double gates which enclosed the driveway, then his car revving before he drove off. Michelle knew that the front door wouldn't be locked as Jacques would have merely pulled it closed as he left, but she was surprised that there was no clunk from the gates closing. It amazed her that he'd installed the gates to stop any of his precious cars being driven away and stolen, yet the house with all her precious contents was left unprotected. It was clear where his priorities lay. Now she was fully awake having been able to grab an extra hour of blissful slumber once all had eventually become quiet once again.

Michelle had planned the perfect day. She'd made a list in her head of her regime for the next few hours, making full use of the trappings of wealth she enjoyed. There was her beautiful swimming pool, the hot-tub, the sauna and enough creams and lotions to satisfy the whole town. Everyone knew that her home was sensational, because Michelle constantly reminded them. She wasn't liked, many hated her, but all were rather frightened of her and that's the way she liked it.

Michelle Moliner enjoyed being rich. She loved the power of wealth. Apart from the mayor's wife, who she considered to be her equal, Michelle thought she was probably the most important woman in the area. But she didn't always hold the position she now enjoyed. As a child, being the fourth daughter of a local cheese merchant, she was way down the pecking order. But Michelle was smart – smart enough to realise the value of marrying well. Jacques Moliner was not as clever as Michelle, but he was an only son and his father was blessed with amazing luck and the ability to turn muck into brass. Jacques' father amassed a huge fortune then conveniently died young, leaving everything divided equally between his wife and his only son. Within one month of her husband's demise, Madame Moliner suffered a massive heart attack and was promptly buried beside him. Jacques didn't grieve for long however; his bulging bank account soon helped to dry his tears.

He'd always liked Michelle, although on and off he'd dated her sister, Helene. In fact, everyone expected him to one day marry Helene. Michelle was petite and pretty, and being rather shy, Jacques appreciated the cute young woman who found him so fascinating. She persuaded him to end things once and for all with Helene, then tempted him with the promise of dirty sex – but only after they were married, of course. Helene was not pleased but there was nothing she could do. Michelle had hooked Jacques, as easily as if he'd jumped on the line and played dead.

Everyone suspected that Michelle found the money more attractive than the man. They all said – those wagging-tongued, jealous bitches – that it wouldn't last and many prayed for the opportunity of stepping into Michelle's shoes. And they were partly right. The sex didn't last and neither did the promise of love ever after, but they underestimated Michelle's tenacity. There was no way she would leave Jacques, not while one single centime remained in the bank account they shared. So the couple continued to live together, yet apart, in the fabulous house they jointly owned, and while Jacques frequently travelled away with the vintage car club, Michelle entertained her current lover and spent more and more of their joint cash, while all of her own earnings were being saved in a secret account in Spain.

But none of that mattered any more. Michelle was beyond caring. One callous act, one murderous act had ended her life and everything she'd worked for.

* * *

When I received the call from the dispatcher, I responded immediately. Accompanied by my assistant Laurent, I left the office and we drove to Michelle Moliner's house. Laurent was excited to be going with me. He, like many others, had speculated about Madame Moliner's home. Only a privileged few; her inner circle, her employees and her husband's close friends, had ever been invited to enter through the large iron security gates and be welcomed at the *castel.*

But, forgive me please, I am rambling on before we have been formally introduced. Allow me to rectify that. My name is Danielle and I am the senior police officer in charge of this region. I oversee my small town, which is situated on the French side of the Eastern Pyrenees. I also look after several villages and farms, quite a large area, in fact. I'm smart and in my thirties – still quite young – but it's been a struggle to reach the esteemed position I now enjoy. Women do not usually reach the higher echelons here and in particular, women who are young and unmarried.

I live with my friend Patricia in a lovely home on the edge of town. It is close enough for me to walk to work, but far enough away from the gossipers and the prying eyes. Not that I have anything to hide, our friendship is that of sisters even though Patricia is a lesbian, but you know how people like to talk.

Anyway, I am rambling again. Apart from Guy Legler, who was Michelle's lover, Laurent and I were the first to arrive at the scene. We found Monsieur Legler in a state of deep shock and no wonder, the sight that greeted us was ghastly. I have never seen a person cooked before and I hope I never witness such a thing again. Within a few minutes the medical emergency team arrived, closely followed by the *pompiers*, who are both firemen and trained paramedics. There is nothing anyone can do. Michelle has been dead for several hours.

I arrange for Monsieur Legler to be taken to the clinic for treatment and send the medical emergency team away. I tell Laurent to return to the office. He is not happy about being dismissed, as he'd like time to look around this house, but that's too bad. I am the boss and he must do as he is told. Besides, he is a bungler, a bit of a buffoon and he irritates me.

I wait at the house with my old friend Jean, who oversees the *pompiers*. We have attended many scenes of death before, and apart from the unfortunate circumstances of our meetings, we enjoy spending the time together, passing a few hours chatting. We must wait now for a medical examiner to attend the corpse before we can move on. My old friend, Doctor Poullet has been summoned, but we have no idea when he will arrive.

Jean and I sit in the landscaped garden in the sunshine and discuss the pétanque club's forthcoming barbecue and the cycle race which is being held next month and the poor condition of the main road through town and indeed, anything else that springs to mind as we await the good doctor's arrival.

Chapter 2

After some time, Poullet's Renault Mégane Estate comes into view and Jean and I reluctantly rise from our comfortable chairs. We watch, cringing, as Poullet manoeuvres his car along the near-empty driveway and parks haphazardly, narrowly missing a large plant pot.

"The silly old fool still can't park, I see," Jean says. "Do you see that bump on his door? He did that at Céret market on Sunday when he tried to squeeze into a space beside a metal bin."

"I have to agree with you there, Jean," I reply. "I always recognise his car when he's in town. It's the one abandoned at a crazy angle. At least his driving is alright. To my knowledge, he's never had an accident."

The driver's door is pushed open and two plump legs appear, feet planted firmly on the gravel driveway. Then gripping the side of the car, Poullet hauls his bulk out and stands. He has never been a thin man, but he is now fatter than ever. Poullet's wife owns a patisserie and it is clear that the good doctor has over indulged in her wares. He waddles towards us.

"I see, once again, you two are enjoying a break sitting in the sunshine while the rest of us work," he says grumpily. "Please, don't let me disturb you. In fact, why not return to your chairs and we can all sit in the sunshine? Perhaps we can have some iced tea or a *pain-au-chocolat*. I'm sure my next patient won't mind waiting," he adds sarcastically.

I am about to protest that there was nothing we could do until he arrived, but it is a waste of time and effort. Poullet always believes his time is more important than everyone else's.

"Well now," he continues. "What's this all about? I've been asked to attend, but nobody has had the courtesy to tell me what's happened. We all know Michelle very well. Has there been an accident?"

Jean and I exchange glances. The doctor is meant to tell us what has occurred, not the other way around, but in this instance, we already know Michelle has been murdered. There can be no other explanation.

"Come inside," I say. "It will be easier once you see the situation of the body."

Poullet stares at us, and purses his lips as if he has a bad taste in his mouth. "Humph," he utters, then shaking his head with annoyance, he marches towards the front door of the house, his heavy footsteps crunching on the gravel.

We enter the house and make our way towards the back where the sauna is situated. It is conveniently placed to allow its user to step out of the wooden box and in a few paces, exit through a glazed door and plunge into the swimming pool.

Although the heat has been switched off, there is an overwhelming stuffiness in the air and a pungent smell, a mixture of sweat and excrement and something indefinable, but reminiscent of cooked pork. Michelle's skin looks shiny and plump, as if all the creases have been ironed out.

"Oh, mon Dieu," Poullet says. He looks shocked. "Poor Michelle, what a terrible way to die! She must have been terrified."

He stares at a sturdy, forked, wooden pole which is lying on the floor.

"Someone wedged that under the door handle," Jean explains. "There was no way she could push the door open. It was held fast."

"Then the killer turned up the heat," I add. "The dial was at one hundred and forty degrees Celsius when I arrived. The murderer fried her brains. He or she wanted Michelle to suffer. I'm pretty sure this wasn't a random act."

"Who would want to do such a thing?" the doctor asks.

"Come, come, Poullet," I reply. "You and I both know Michelle was not liked. There will be many people delighted to see the back of her. The list will be as long as your arm."

"Yes, that's true," he agrees. "Many would want to be watching and knitting as the guillotine fell, but who would be angry enough or desperate enough to release the blade, I wonder?"

It is now quite late in the day and I cannot do any more here, so I say goodbye to Jean and drive back towards my office. Someone must inform Jacques Moliner of his wife's death, but first we'll have to locate him. Doctor Poullet told me that Jacques is a member of the vintage car club and they are holding a rally this weekend and he is not expected to return until late on Sunday evening. I telephone ahead and set Laurent the task of finding his mobile phone number. I ask my other assistant, Paul, to call the clinic and see if Guy Legler has recovered sufficiently for me to question him. As he found the body, he and Jacques are the prime suspects for Michelle's murder. Personally, I don't believe they had anything to do with the killing, but nevertheless their alibis must be checked out.

From what has been rumoured, Jacques knew that Michelle had a lover, but turned a blind eye to the affair and the several she'd had in the past. I can't understand what men saw in Michelle. She was scrawny, had a pinched face, a narrow little mouth full of sharp rat-like teeth and a tongue that could cut you with one phrase. I disliked the woman intensely and I was not alone.

Being the local estate agent and a close friend of the *notaire* she was in a very powerful position. Many people accused her of ripping off her clients, particularly the ex-pat community who are vulnerable and easy pickings, although nobody really cares about them. More disturbingly, there have been several dubious deals recently, involving local people. Conspiracy theories have been suggested and knowing Michelle and Pascal Boutiere, the *notaire*, I'm afraid they might well be true. I am not looking forward to interviewing potential murder suspects, as I think they could form a very long list.

Chapter 3

When I arrive back at the office, Paul and Laurent are amusing each other by telling sick jokes about Michelle's death. For some reason, ghastly events always inspire such humour. I enter my office and within a couple of minutes Paul brings me a coffee and news about Guy Legler and Jacques Moliner. Paul is a handsome devil with a cheeky smile, and he's smart, much smarter than Laurent. He places the coffee on my desk along with a slice of apricot cake.

"I thought you'd probably want something sweet after your baked lunch," he says. I grimace and he relents. "You look a bit pale, Boss. I imagine it was pretty awful."

"Not a pretty sight," I agree. "But I guess Michelle wasn't especially beautiful at the best of times," I add.

Paul smiles. "Let me update you," he says. "Michelle has a studio apartment that she rents in town. Guy Legler has a key to this apartment and some of his belongings are kept there. His main residence is in Cadaqués, over the border in Spain. He calls himself a property agent, but he's not registered or legally connected to any agency as far as I can see. I suspect he's more like an introducer than an agent. I think he homed in on Michelle because she was successful and had money. Legler is considerably younger than her and much better looking. The clinic has released him, but he's been treated for shock and we can't question him for at least twenty-four hours. He's been told to stay in town and this is his address."

Paul hands me a piece of paper and I am surprised to see that the studio is in a building jointly owned by Monsieur Claude, our esteemed spa owner, and my dear friend Patricia. I had no idea Michelle was renting an apartment there and I'm sure Patricia doesn't know either. The building was meant to provide high-priced, luxury accommodation for 'curists' having treatments at the spa. It will be interesting to see how much Michelle is paying for its use, but I'd bet it's not nearly enough.

"Jacques is in Figueres with his car club," Paul says. "He's been informed of his wife's death by the local police, but none of his group are able to drive tonight, because after they arrived there and booked into their hotel, they spent the rest of the day drinking. He's planning to return tomorrow afternoon."

"There's no point sending a car for him, as there's nothing any of us can do today. I think we can take tomorrow off as normal and speak to Guy and Jacques on Monday when they are in a better state of mind."

"I agree, Boss. We can't interview a drunk."

"So, Michelle's lover came up from Spain as her husband travelled down," I say. "How convenient. I'll send a one-liner by email to Detective Gerard in Perpignan to advise him what's happened, then we'll finish up here. Laurent is on call tomorrow and I see no reason to change that arrangement."

We are discussing the rest of the list of people we'll need to interview when we hear a rabble of voices coming from the main office.

"We'd better see what's going on," I say to Paul. "It's nearly close of day and we can look at this again on Monday when we're fresh. It's going to take a bit of planning."

The noise is getting louder and when I open the door I see several familiar faces, all of them acquaintances of Michelle. Bad news travels fast, it seems.

"*Messieurs et Mesdames*, can I be of assistance? Is there a problem here?"

They all begin to speak at once.

"Is it true? Is Michelle dead? Has she been murdered? Did Jacques kill her? I heard she was burned to death in a fire? What will happen to her business, she's holding a deposit for me? Is it safe?"

I hold up my hands in a placatory fashion. "Please," I say. "I can't hear you when you're all speaking at once." They stop talking and I begin to explain. "Michelle Moliner was found dead earlier today. She died in the sauna at her home. We suspect she's been murdered, but we'll know more when we get the doctor's report. There was no fire. I cannot comment on her business. You'll have to speak to someone in her office about that. There is nothing more I can tell you now, and as we are about to lock up, I'd be grateful if you would all leave."

They begin to mutter once again, showing no signs of leaving.

"Please," I say. "Have you no homes to go to?" Reluctantly, they shuffle through the door chatting to each other, and I'm certain they all have a theory. All except Monsieur Claude – he alone is silent and when the others leave, he remains.

"Yes, Claude," I say. "Is there something more? Can't it wait until Monday?"

"I suppose it will keep, Danielle, but I think you'll want to speak to me. I have some information, one or two things that might be important."

Paul looks pointedly at his watch. "Can Laurent and I leave now, Boss? There's a meeting of the pétanque club tonight and we're already late."

I look at the clock. We should have left ten minutes ago.

"We'll all leave," I say. "I'll walk with you as far as my car Claude, and we can agree on a time to have a chat, but let's leave it until Monday afternoon please. I plan to spend what's left of the weekend with Patricia and Monday morning is always busy."

I am curious to hear what he has to say about Michelle, but I feel no sense of urgency on Claude's part, so it can wait. In the end, he chooses not to walk with me because he too, is attending the pétanque meeting and I watch as all three men race away towards the riverside venue.

I find it difficult to come to terms with having to deal with yet another death in my area. This used to be such a quiet place. Maybe it has something to do with global warming, I speculate. Maybe people are simply becoming more volatile and hot-headed.

Chapter 4

I wake on Sunday morning to the sun streaming in through a chink in the curtains. It is early, but already warm. I can hear Patricia moving about downstairs. She is singing and her sweet voice is melodious. Every so often, I hear her scolding our dog Ollee, who is obviously getting under her feet. I know, even before I descend the stairs, that there will be pans of fruit bubbling on the stove as she prepares her preserves for the market. Next weekend is the bullfight *feria* in the neighbouring town of Céret and people will travel from far and wide to attend.

Being north Catalonia, we have a tradition of bullfighting in our region. It used to be a very popular event on both sides of the border, but recently Spanish Catalonia has banned the spectacle. We in the north have benefited greatly from this, as all the money now pours into Céret and into our pockets instead of Spain's.

This year Patricia will have two points of sale. One stall, which is to sell preserves and pickles, will be manned by her friend Sarah. Sarah is raising money for the protection of cats and is happy to work for a small donation to her cause. Sarah is the absolute authority on all things feathered, fluffy or furry. She is rather odd, but her heart is in the right place. The other stall will be manned by Patricia herself. She has produced over forty small paintings with scenes from bullfights, which she will sell at fifty euros each. They each took only a short time to paint as they are simple depictions, but they give the impression of colour and movement and I'm sure she'll sell them all.

This year I do not have to work on the *feria* weekend so I'm planning to attend at least one of the bullfights. My good friend Byron will accompany me and I'm delighted. For an English gentleman, he makes a very acceptable Frenchman.

On this occasion, our dog Ollee will have to stay at home. He won't be pleased but it will be safer for him and besides, he rather enjoys lying on his blanket in the sunshine. He is a brave and game dog, but no match for a running bull, or for that matter, a reeling drunk and there will be plenty of them at the *feria*. Many children are not as spoiled as our dog. Patricia indulges his every whim and he adores her.

Because I knew Patricia would be busy this morning, I've arranged to go with Byron to a *vide grenier*, a car boot sale, in Perpignan. Byron likes to dabble in the trade of antiques and he's always on the lookout for a bargain. This sale is only held in the morning and when I look at my watch, I see I'll have to get a move on as he's due to arrive in twenty minutes.

"There's coffee in the jug and croissants on the table," Patricia says when I enter the kitchen.

Before I manage my first bite, Ollee is barking and Byron is at the door.

"Come in Byron," Patricia calls as she spies him through the window. "It's not locked."

"You must have smelled the coffee," I say, when he enters the room.

"And the croissants," he replies. "I'll join you for a quick cup if you don't mind. We've got a few minutes. I'm a bit early."

"Help yourself," I offer and pass him a mug and a plate. "The croissants are really good or there's baguette if you prefer."

"You are too good to me, dear girl," he replies.

"Yes, I am," I agree and he laughs and winks at me.

Although Byron is an older man – closer to my father's age than to mine, in fact – he is very charismatic and I find him attractive. Being tall and having a lean frame with long elegant limbs, he wears his clothes well. Today he is dressed in white linen. His shirt is almost transparent as it is so fine and a soft, dark blue, cashmere sweater is draped casually around his shoulders. Everything about him oozes class.

"What are you looking for today?" Patricia asks and she joins us at the table for a couple of minutes.

"Anything that will make me money and will fit into Danielle's car, I'm not too choosy, to be honest. Of course, I dream about finding gold priced as base metal or a Chippendale chair which hasn't been constructed by 'Chip and Dale', but it's a long shot. Most people know the value of their goods and yet they still overcharge," he replies, laughing. "But one can live in hope, dear girl. You just never know, I might get lucky – besides, we'll have an enjoyable morning pottering about."

"And we'll be out of your way," I add.

"I won't complain about that," Patricia says, "if you promise to look out for any glass jars that I can use for bottling fruit. They've become so expensive to buy new. I'll take any quantity you can find, even if there's only one or two. I've been storing them up for weeks so I'm ready for the autumn harvest," she explains to Byron. "Danielle's papa says we'll have a bumper crop this year and I've already secured several orders for apricots in brandy for Christmas."

"Christmas orders in July, eh?" Byron says. "Business must be good." He turns to me, "Everything still working out with your dad then? He's still enjoying working for you girls at the orchard? I thought the arrangement was only supposed to be for a few months, but it's been quite a while now."

"He says he loves that orchard and he'll never retire," I reply. "In fact, he morbidly told me that if he dies on the job we're simply to dig a hole and plant him with his beloved trees."

Byron laughs. "On that charming note, we'd better get going," he suggests, stuffing the final bit of a croissant into his mouth and wiping his lips with his handkerchief. "The bargains are waiting and my money is burning a hole in my pocket."

It takes us half an hour to reach the place where the '*vide grenier*' is being held and, as we approach, we can see that the area set aside for the stalls is filled to bursting point. Because it is early, there are still one or two parking spaces available in the main car park, although most have been taken by the stall holders after they've unloaded their goods onto the stalls. I manage to manoeuvre my car into a narrow space between a white van and a covered trailer, beside one of the exits.

"Well done, Danielle," Byron says approvingly. "This is a great space and it's so close to the section of the sale that I especially want to look at. Only about a quarter of the stalls have old stuff, the rest are traders hoping to sell new goods; a person can buy anything here from beetroot to barnacles if they want."

"Not too many people wanting to buy barnacles, I imagine," I reply. "But I bet Patricia could make use of the beetroot."

"You never know, Danielle. People buy the strangest things. Which is just as well, or I wouldn't have a business," he observes. "Anyway, let's get going before more speculators arrive. After rising at an ungodly hour and coming all this way, I don't want to miss anything."

He's like an excited child as he rushes through the entrance. I personally would much rather take a gentle stroll so we decide to split up and meet again in an hour.

"I'll phone your mobile if I need your assistance, but otherwise, let's meet at the food van and I'll buy you a coffee," he says.

I can already smell the food van. I can't understand why, but there's something enticing about the aroma of greasy sausages that's hard to resist. Even at this early hour, a queue has formed and people are munching on baguettes stuffed with all manner of fried, fatty offerings.

Most of the tables have junk for sale. People are enthusing about everything from empty YSL lipstick containers to chipped plates. There's a whole mishmash of clutter and I don't know how Byron will be able to separate his 'little gems' from this rubbish. By the time I've looked at four or five stalls, I'm bored. There is a minor argument when one vendor accuses his neighbour of stealing one of his offerings and hiding it under his own table, but all is quickly resolved when the wife of the first man explains that she sold it when her husband went to the toilet. Other than that incident, it is a very quiet affair, and although we are outside, there is a feeling of calm, almost a reverence about the place, like being in church. I suspect it's the lull before the storm and I'm sure in another hour or so, the place will come alive with families and will become a heaving mass of noise and pushing and shoving.

I am about halfway through my tour of the place when I see one of the jars Patricia is looking for. It is at the back of a rather cluttered table, so I ask the stallholder to pass it to me for examination. I fear, if I reach for it, many of the other items might come crashing down. After a couple of minutes of praising the functionality of the jar I am informed by the seller that he has another nine of them under the stall and they are unused.

"My wife is always starting another hobby," the seller explains. "One day she is going to be an artist and within a few weeks, I'll be selling art equipment. Another day I might have sewing accoutrements or baking tins. I've even had woodworking tools. But today glass jars for bottling fruit. You can have the whole lot for two euros and I'll be glad to be rid of them as they take up so much room."

I'm delighted and Patricia will be thrilled, as these jars are usually very expensive. I quickly pay for my purchase then ferry them back to my car before resuming my search. My find has lifted my flagging spirits and I'm feeling less bored.

I have almost completed one circuit of the place when I spot Byron at an adjacent stall. He is holding the ugliest vase I have ever seen. It looks like a decorated brick. He is trying to look barely interested in the object but I can see his eyes are bright and sparkling and I recognise that look, because I've seen it before and I know he's discovered something of value. I keep glancing over and I see that there are two, similar ugly vases in front of him. He is chatting to the stall holder and they are laughing. Now the man is wrapping up the items in newspaper and Byron has a twenty euro note in his hand. I'm trying not to stare, but I'm intrigued. I personally wouldn't have given these horrible bits of pottery a second glance, but Byron obviously has some knowledge of their worth. As he leaves the stall with his purchases, I walk over to him.

"Found something good?" I enquire.

"Yes, a little gem; three of them in fact. Let's get our coffees and I'll show you," he replies.

We make our way to the food van and Byron places his package on a table in front of me and goes to fetch the drinks. When he returns, he carefully unwraps the vases and sits them on the table. To me, they still look like decorated bricks.

"They're Troika," he explains. "From Cornwall in England and they're worth a small fortune. These two," he says, pointing to the taller vases, "are worth about a hundred pounds each. But this round one will easily sell for two to three hundred. I plan to sell them on eBay and I bet they'll be purchased by someone in the UK. The seller told me he bought them in a job lot when he was clearing a house and his wife hates them."

"I can understand why," I reply. "Who would want these ugly vases in their home? And who would pay that sort of money for them?"

"As we said before, people buy the strangest things and that's why I have this little business. I have the knowledge you see, and knowledge is power."

I fold my arms, sit back in my chair and relax. Byron is right I think. Knowledge is power and I am blessed with both.

Chapter 5

When I arrive at my office on Monday morning I'm shocked to see Detective Gerard waiting at the door. He almost never comes here and I wonder if I've done something wrong. I feel a prickle of anxiety and a film of perspiration forms between my skin and my clothes. As I approach, he looks at his watch.

"I see you're an early bird too," he says and a quick smile passes over his lips. "I've already been to see Jacques Moliner. When we get inside I'll tell you all about it."

Oh, *merde*, I think. I was due to see Jacques this morning. Does Gerard think I can't do my job? I unlock the door and show him straight through into my office. Paul arrives at my heels.

"Coffee, now please," I say, "and some biscuits from the tin."

Paul's face is serious. He raises his eyebrows and gives me a questioning look. I shrug, I don't know any more than him at this stage.

Gerard and I sit at opposite sides of my desk and within a couple of minutes Paul places the coffees in front of us then leaves and shuts the door behind him. I wait for Detective Gerard to say something. He infuriates me by making me wait while he gulps down some coffee. I don't want to be the first to speak, so I bite my tongue and try not to sigh.

Eventually, he begins. "You're probably wondering why I'm here and why I went to see Jacques." He pauses and stares straight into my eyes, as if searching for something. I wait and hold his gaze. "Jacques Moliner is my cousin," he finally reveals. "He's devastated by Michelle's death. I thought it would be easier if I spoke to him first. You do understand don't you, Danielle? He's my cousin and he called me."

I am angry. It's against all procedure in a murder enquiry. Being a relative, Gerard should have distanced himself from this case, not been the first to speak to the main suspect. I am appalled.

"When did you hear about Michelle?" I ask.

"Jacques telephoned me from Figueres as soon as he heard. And then, of course, I saw your email."

So, I think, Jacques was sober enough to phone Detective Gerard for assistance, but was too drunk to get himself home by any means.

"I plan to interview Jacques today, this morning in fact," I say. "Do you have any objection? Are you planning to take over this case?"

"Oh, no, no, of course not, it's your case. I'm only here to support my family. I wouldn't dream of interfering."

"And how did you find Jacques? Is he in a fit state to be interviewed?" I ask.

"It's a terrible business, I'm afraid, Michelle suffered a horrible death. I knew her quite well and I know her sister Helene, too."

"You're right, it's shocking. Jacques is understandably very upset, but he did confide in me that although he and Michelle were close, they were no longer lovers. They stayed together, because being devout Catholics, neither could contemplate divorce. He said they were very content and I believe him."

"Who's with him now? He's not on his own, is he?"

"No, no, Helene is with him. She's going to stay at the house for a few days and help with any arrangements. Michelle's assistant Marie will run the office in the meantime. They can't close at the height of the tourist and 'curist' season. They can't let the clients down."

"Helene is unmarried so she's got no other dependants to look after. I'm sure she'll be a great help to Jacques at this difficult time," I say.

"Absolutely," Gerard replies.

"What are your plans, Sir? Are you planning to stay in town for a while?"

"No, Danielle, it's really busy in the city at the moment and I'm confident you'll handle everything in your usual professional fashion, so I'm heading back to Perpignan this afternoon. I'm satisfied that Jacques had nothing to do with Michelle's death and I'm sure you'll reach the same conclusion once you've taken everyone's statements."

I can't help feeling that I've just been given an order, rather than an opinion and I'm not happy about it. If I don't solve this case it will look bad on my record, but if all the evidence points to Jacques as the murderer, I can kiss my career progression goodbye. I seem to be between a rock and a hard place and I sincerely hope someone – anyone, other than Jacques, killed Michelle.

After some chit-chat, Detective Gerard leaves my office. I walk him to the front door then watch him as he gets into his car. It's a relief to see him drive off.

"What on earth was that all about?" Paul asks. "The Big Boss never comes here. Have we done something wrong? What has Laurent fucked up this time?" he asks, glancing towards his colleague.

Laurent is about to protest then clamps his lips firmly shut and I suspect there could be all manner of things he's messed up that he doesn't want me to know about.

"We haven't done anything wrong. Detective Gerard is Jacques Moliner's cousin. He's been to see him."

"Oh, I see. Oh, merde. We're in the spotlight then," Paul replies.

"What if Jacques killed his wife? Where would that leave us? We won't be very popular if we charge the Big Boss's cousin with murder," Laurent says.

I guess Laurent has more brains than I give him credit for; even he can see the predicament we face.

Chapter 6

Before I go to the Moliner house I telephone Pierre, who is our forensic expert. He tells me that he's now released the site but he has virtually nothing to report.

"The forked stick that was used to secure the door is covered in grease, animal fat actually," he says. "There are fingerprints, but mostly smudges, and so many it looks as if half the town have had their hands on it. It has marks on its base as if it's been clamped at sometime, but I've no idea why."

"Do you think the killer or killers brought it with them?" I ask. "It's obviously been used for something before."

"I don't know. It's quite a large object to be carrying unnoticed. I suggest you ask Jacques Moliner if he's seen it around his property. The killer must have known prior to arriving, that this particular prop would fit and secure the door, which leads me to believe they've been to the house before."

Pierre promises to send me a report and I end the call. Then I summon Paul and we leave the office to go and interview Jacques.

When I drive through the magnificent iron gates and park on the gravel driveway, Paul can't help commenting about the opulence of the place.

"Wow," he says. "I've heard so much about the *castel* but I had no idea it would be so beautiful. Those stairs leading to the front door are Italian marble and the garden is absolutely stunning. I didn't know Madame Moliner had such good taste."

"She didn't," I say. "According to what I've heard, all the finishing touches to this place were the work of her sister, Helene. She's the one with good taste. Michelle simply supplied the money and of course, enjoyed the fruits of Helene's labour."

"But Helene doesn't live here, does she? I know she's unmarried, where does she live?"

"The spinster sister is relegated to a modest apartment in town, close to the office. She does most of the grunge work along with Marie, the secretary, while Michelle enjoyed the fast life."

"I guess some people are destined to be downtrodden victims," Paul says. "Who actually owns the business? Does Helene have any part of it? Will she gain from Michelle's death?"

"Good question Paul, we can ask that when we interview her."

We crunch our way along the gravel path and I'm about to ring the doorbell when the door is opened by Helene. She is a short, slightly plump lady with a pleasant heart-shaped face; even dressed in black, she looks wholesome. There is sweetness in her smile which immediately makes us feel welcome.

"I saw you drive up," she explains. "You were expected, that's why Jacques had the gates open. Then I heard your car on the gravel."

Helene shows us into the lounge. When I was here on Saturday I hadn't really noticed how richly furnished the place is because I was preoccupied with more urgent matters, but as sunlight streams through the large windows, Paul let's out an audible gasp. Although the minimalist style is not entirely to my taste, the spacious room is filled with light. Large pictures, colourful depictions of paintings by Monet, adorn the walls, increasing the feeling of space. It is cool, even though the day is hot and I can't help thinking how pleasant it must have been for Michelle to live in such a place. Helene asks us to sit down and we sink into a plush leather sofa. Almost immediately, Jacques enters the room and he sits opposite us in an armchair. He looks as if he's just stepped out of the shower, his skin is glowing and his hair is wet.

"I'll just fetch some coffee," Helene offers and she scurries out of the room.

"I am very sorry for your loss, Jacques," I say and Paul mumbles the same platitude.

"Thank you, Danielle," Jacques replies and he nods an acknowledgment to Paul. "It's been such a terrible shock." He pauses then says, "Before you ask, I'll tell you, Michelle and I were no longer intimate. I knew all about her lovers and I accepted that this was our way of life. I too had other friends. But I loved my wife, I've always loved her and I can't believe someone could do this to her. Have you spoken to Guy Legler yet?" he asks, changing the subject. "I don't trust that man. There's something shifty about him – he can't look you straight in the eye."

"Perhaps he can't look you in the eye, Jacques," I reply. "Perhaps he was embarrassed by his affair with Michelle."

"No, I don't think it's that. We both knew the situation. I think the man is a liar and, besides, he was the only person here. I was in Figueres when he called for assistance."

"Jacques," I say softly. "You and I both know that Michelle had many enemies. Some people were jealous of her good fortune and others blamed her for their business problems. I cannot simply assume that Guy Legler is the culprit, however much you dislike him."

Helene arrives with a tray which she sets down on the coffee table. We sit in silence as she fills four cups and soon we are sipping the delicious, nutty-flavoured brew.

"I can take my coffee in the kitchen if you'd rather speak to Jacques in private," she offers.

"I'd like Helene to stay, if that's okay," Jacques says and I nod my acceptance.

I begin to question Jacques and Paul takes notes. Before very long, I have established the exact time he rose on that fateful morning, the time he left for Figueres and that he had conducted no conversation with Michelle before he left the house. As the forked stick used to secure the door had been removed before he arrived home, Jacques couldn't comment on it.

"As far as I was aware, Michelle was still asleep when I left," he says.

"Did you lock the door behind you?" I ask.

"I can't actually remember," he replies. "I certainly pulled it closed, but I'm not sure if I turned the key in the lock. I can't swear either way."

"So anyone could have entered the house."

Jacques shrugs. "Perhaps, but I doubt it. Who would be around here at that time on a Saturday morning? We are quite out of the way. What time did Legler say he got here?"

"That's irrelevant, Jacques. If the door wasn't locked, we can't rule out a stranger entering the house."

"But nothing has been stolen. Why would a stranger enter my house and kill my wife? What reason could they possibly have?" Jacques voice has risen and he is becoming rather distressed.

"Jacques," Helene says gently, placing her hand over his. "Calm down. Don't upset yourself, the officer is simply doing her duty. She's not blaming you. Even if you didn't lock the door, none of this is your fault. Only the person who committed the crime is to blame."

Jacques noticeably relaxes. "Yes, yes, you're right Helene, I'm sorry, I'm really sorry. I still can't believe this has happened." A sob escapes from his throat and he covers his face with his hands.

I turn my attention to Helene. "Where were you on Saturday?" I ask. "Were you anywhere near this house?"

Her face flushes because I've caught her unawares with the question.

"Me, on Saturday? You want to know where I was? Do you really think I had something to do with this?"

"I don't want to upset you," I say. "But I must take statements from anyone and everyone who had access to this house. I assume you have a key?"

"Yes, of course I do," she concedes. "But so have many other people. Anyway, on Saturday I opened the office then I spent the day inspecting some of the empty houses that we're trying to sell. Marie, the secretary, can confirm I left that morning with a bunch of keys. I have a list of potential buyers and I don't like showing a house until I know it looks okay to be viewed, so I make sure it's clean and tidy, that sort of thing."

"You said other people have keys, can you tell me who?"

Helene and Jacques exchange glances. "There's a set of keys in Michelle's desk drawer in the office, so Marie has access and therefore so does her husband, Franck."

"Franck does gardening work for us and I sometimes give him my spare set of keys so he has access to water," Jacques adds. "Then there's Guy, who you already know about. He could have had a copy made and given it to someone else. As I said before, I don't trust the man, and as you know, he wasn't the first of Michelle's lovers to visit this house."

"Anyone who Michelle has lent her key chain to, could have had access," Helene says. "Sometimes she let her friends use her garage in town. I know for a fact that Monsieur Claude, the spa owner and Pascal Boutiere, the *notaire* used it on several occasions. Michelle would simply hand over her bunch of keys to them."

"I see," I reply. "So lots people have, or have had keys. That was very relaxed. Weren't you frightened of being robbed, Jacques?"

"We have the iron gates, so I didn't really consider it," he replies.

I've come to the end of my questions and I don't think I'll get any more useful information from either of them today, so I nod to Paul and we get up to leave.

"Thank you for the coffee, Helene," I say. "Once again, I'm so sorry for your loss. I'll be in touch when I know anything more or if I need to talk to either of you again. Oh, but there are just two more questions and I'm sorry to have to ask this. Did Michelle own the business outright? And who is the beneficiary of her will?"

"It's Michelle's business and I'm her beneficiary," Jacques states. "No one else will benefit. Which means nobody had a reason to kill her."

Helene purses her lips and stares at her feet and it's clear she is not going to add to his statement. Paul and I exchange handshakes with the pair, then Jacques walks us to the door as Helene busies herself with the tray.

"You'd better get your locks changed," I suggest. "We don't know who did this terrible thing, but they're still out there and they might be very dangerous."

A look of shock passes over Jacques' face – he obviously hadn't considered that the killer might return. Paul and I leave him standing in the doorway and we crunch back along the path to the car.

"Do you think perhaps Michelle wasn't the only target, Boss? Do you think the killer will come back for Jacques?"

"No," I reply. "I believe Michelle was indeed the target, but it's better to be safe than sorry. Besides, Jacques's shocked reaction to my suggestion let's me know that he did not kill his wife."

Chapter 7

By the time we get back to the office, it's practically lunchtime and I ask Paul and Laurent to decide which of them will go out first, leaving the other to hold the fort. I intend to visit the café, in the hope of seeing Patricia. She told me she'd eat there today because she's coming into town to check on the apartment Guy Legler has been using. Although he has a key, Michelle was the client. In fact, Patricia said that she and Claude intend to ask Legler to vacate the apartment later today, because he doesn't have any right to remain. I want to ask her to wait until after five o'clock, to give me time to interview him before he disappears back to Cadaqués.

As I walk along the main street where the café is situated, I read the menu boards outside each establishment that provides lunches. There are four different formula meals on offer today and any one of them would be acceptable to me. However, the warm duck salad advertised on the café's board looks particularly inviting and who could resist *tarte-au-citron* for dessert? I see Patricia sitting at a table near the door and when she notices me she waves and smiles.

"Bonjour, Danielle, I'm so pleased you could manage to come. It's a lovely day and the menu looks very good. Oh, and Byron is here too. He's just taken Ollee for a little walk. There he is now," she says, without drawing breath.

Byron approaches and before I can sit down Ollee hurtles towards me, jumping up and planting slobbery kisses in my ear and on my cheek.

"Stop! Sit down, you stupid dog," I shout. He dives under the table, almost tipping it over, then jumps onto a seat, barking and wagging his tail.

"I guess he's as pleased to see you, as I am," Byron says. "But don't worry, dear girl. I've no intention of jumping up and licking your ear."

"Well thank goodness for that," Patricia says, pushing the dog off the seat and steering him under the table. "One love-struck boy is quite enough," she adds and we all laugh.

"I'm hardly a boy, but thanks for the compliment, dear girl. You know that I do love you both very much."

"Oh, stop being such a soppy old fool, Byron," I say and we find ourselves laughing again.

The waiter arrives at our table and places a pitcher of ice cold water and a basket of fresh bread in front of us. As we are all having the formula menu, we order at once.

"And *le chien*, do you have a water bowl for him? Will he be dining too?" he asks.

"Ollee won't be having a meal today, thank you," Patricia says. "But I have a bowl for him if you wouldn't mind bringing some more water."

"*Certainement*," the waiter replies and disappears back inside.

Byron chuckles. "I've lived in this town for years and I still can't get my head around the restaurant service being offered to dogs. In England, a dog can't enter a restaurant, but in this town, they're served at the table. It's ridiculous – crazy, but charming. No wonder the Brits think we're all mad here. France makes all these strict rules for Europe, but only the British obey them. It's crazy, totally crazy."

"But Byron," Patricia protests. "You wouldn't want poor Ollee to be thirsty. It's such a hot day today."

Byron chuckles once more, smiles and shakes his head, "Of course not, dear girl. We can't have that. Indeed not."

The waiter arrives with our food and the conversation pauses as we all tuck in. I'm glad we are seated under the canopy near the entrance because it's so hot today and the shade is very welcoming. The gauge at the pharmacy is already reading twenty-eight degrees and that may yet rise a degree or two as the day progresses. The town is busy because it is now tourist season. Many French people come down from the north to enjoy the good weather and there are also large numbers of British arriving every day. I personally prefer September, when they all go home, but the town benefits from the money they spend, and besides, the holiday season only lasts for two months.

"When are you and Claude seeing Guy Legler?" I ask Patricia, when we have all finished eating our salads.

"We are meeting him at six. Why do you ask?"

"Six is perfect. I want to interview him before you put him out and that will give me time to see him in the apartment."

"Is there a problem, Danielle? Some reason to interview him there, rather than the office?"

"No problem," I reply. "I just thought I'd get more out of him there. More about Michelle and his time spent with her. Also, it will let me identify any items that belong to her and remove anything of importance before he gets the chance to disappear back to Spain."

"I have a key, Danielle. I can let you in after lunch, if you'd like," Patricia offers. "He can't complain, because he has no contract with us."

"Thanks, darling, but I don't want to tip him off and give him time to concoct a story. I'd rather catch him unawares. Do you think he'll be at the apartment after lunch?"

"Yes, he said he'd be there all day and if he went out, he'd only be a few minutes."

"Perfect, after lunch I'll go around with one of my boys."

"That sounds ominous," Byron says. "It makes you sound like a Mafia boss. 'Beware Guy Legler. Your number's up. Danielle and her boys are coming to pay you a little visit and if they don't get answers you could end up in the river wearing concrete boots'."

Patricia and I exchange mystified looks. We have no idea what Byron is talking about. It must be his strange English sense of humour.

"You have no idea what I'm on about, do you?" he says. "You French have no sense of humour."

"And you English go out in the midday sun with the mad dogs," I reply.

At the mention of the word dog, Ollee yips.

"See? He knows what I mean," Byron says, laughing. "At least the dog understands me."

"As I said before, English, midday sun and mad dogs," I reply and once again we are laughing.

Chapter 8

I take Laurent with me to talk to Guy Legler. He is not my first choice, but Paul is busy with a tourist family who have bumped their rental car. The husband is red-faced and looks as if he might cry, the wife is badgering him and criticising him, and the children – two girls, both teenagers – are flirting with Paul. Paul's face is sweating and he looks exasperated while Laurent smiles smugly as he and I abandon the poor man to his fate.

"Hah, that'll teach him," Laurent says. "He usually dumps the losers on me, but this time he got stuck with them because I was in the toilet. Serves him right, I'm fed up getting all the rubbish to deal with."

I say nothing. I can't be bothered with pettiness. We arrive at the apartment building and enter. Michelle has rented one of the ground floor studios. I'll find out on what terms exactly, later today, when I speak to Monsieur Claude. I knock on the door and we hear a shuffling sound, as if someone is clearing things away, then the key is turned and the door opened. Guy Legler greets us with a smile and I can understand why Michelle was attracted to him. He is very handsome, with finely-chiselled features and a strong chin. His blue eyes are startling, very bright, like Patricia's. His hair is blonde and his skin golden tan, his frame is tall and muscular. Totally different from Michelle's short, dark, Catalan looks. This man is an Adonis. Michelle was a little rat, but of course, Michelle had money and I suspect Guy Legler is broke.

"Do come in, Officers," he says, wiping the smile from his lips and replacing it with a serious look. "You're here about Michelle," he states. "Awful, awful business, I found her you know. I'll never get that terrible image out of my head. I've had nightmares ever since."

"You probably don't remember us," I say. "My assistant and I were the officers who responded to your call. I arranged for you to be taken to the clinic."

He peers at us. "Yes, I do remember you. Come in, please come in. Sorry about the mess, but I'm packing. I'm being evicted. The heartless couple who own this building are evicting me, even though the rent is fully paid in advance for another month. They'll probably let it again and be paid twice. Michelle would have been so angry."

I smile to myself. Patricia and Claude probably will do exactly that, and I hope, wherever Michelle is now, she is angry – helpless and angry, like many of her clients before.

We sit on the bed in the small studio and Guy sits on the only chair. The apartment is tiny, but very stylish. The wardrobe doors and the drawers of a tall chest are lying open. Guy's belongings, which seem to consist of a suit carrier and a bag of clothing, are already packed and there are a couple of bin bags, presumably full of rubbish, near the door. There is a small combination safe, which is closed, inside the wardrobe. Guy says he's never used it and has never been told the code to open it.

"It could contain anything from fresh air to the British crown jewels, but I wouldn't know. I never saw Michelle use it either," he adds.

I establish that the lovers used this apartment when Jacques was home, but Guy visited Michelle's house when her husband was away. On Saturday, he was intending to arrive at the house in the afternoon and spend the night there, then leave on Sunday morning before Jacques returned from Figueres.

"Michelle paid for the apartment every three months in advance," Guy says. "It wasn't cheap, either. The couple who own it reduced the usual cost by only ten percent and they were supposedly friends of Michelle. Now they're chucking me out and stealing the rent money. It's so unfair," he whines.

"That's life," I reply. "Nobody said it was fair." Laurent nods in agreement and I can't help smirking. Serves you right, I think. You're nothing but a parasite.

We're soon finished with Guy Legler. He has nothing much to tell us and I don't intend to waste my time on him. He's too polished and too handsome and I'm sure that within a week or two, he'll find another lonely, older woman to live off. I'm positive he had nothing to do with Michelle's death. She was his meal ticket, but that particular buffet car has now been closed.

When we return to the office, Claude is sitting at Paul's desk and they are drinking coffee and talking about cars. Both have a passion for expensive cars, but only Claude can afford them.

"Monsieur Claude has a classic Porsche Turbo Coupe," Paul says, obviously impressed. "He says I can be his partner in the car rally next October."

"But just as my navigator," Claude stresses. "I'll be doing all the driving."

Paul is beaming, clearly thrilled to be invited.

"Don't you usually enter these things with Doctor Poullet? Won't he be disappointed?" I ask.

"Pah, that old codger is too fat for my car. He's enormous. Every year he grows bigger and bigger. You'd think a doctor would know better. I don't want the chassis ruined. My beautiful car isn't built for his weight. It's time for new blood, and Paul here is the man for the job."

That may be so," I say. "But who's going to tell Poullet? Anyway Claude, you'd better come into my office. You had something you wanted to tell me."

Claude stands and shakes Paul's hand, then carries his coffee to my room. When we are seated, he begins.

"You'll know by now that Michelle was renting a studio from me and Patricia," he says. "I gave her a ten percent discount because she paid three months in advance, not because we were friends. You'll also know all about her lover," he continues.

"Claude," I interrupt, sighing. "Why don't you tell me something I don't know."

He rubs his hands together nervously before he speaks again. "Michelle has three outstanding court cases against her currently. Some people have accused her of stealing deposits paid over to her company. Michelle explained to me that she merely took her fee from the money paid. She received no deposits. There was never any *compromis de vente* signed at the *notaire*. These people don't have a leg to stand on. Every one of the complainants is a foreigner, so what can one expect? They make a mistake because they don't understand the system then try to blame it on someone else."

"Do you think any of these people had the capability or the inclination to harm Michelle?"

"I just don't know. Many have mouthed off about her, but murder? Who knows what a person will do when they're very angry."

"Who can tell me the names of the people involved? Do you know, Claude?"

"I'm sorry, but no. Perhaps Pascal Boutiere can shed some light on it. He was very close to Michelle, you know. In fact, I wouldn't be surprised if they were having a fling. She always went after younger men, especially men who could benefit her in business."

"The more I hear about Michelle, the more I dislike her."

"Everyone disliked her," Claude says. "In fact, the people closest to her probably hated her the most. She was a bad bitch and most folk will be glad to see the back of her. She even stole Jacques from her sister, you know? Helene was in love with him, but he couldn't resist Michelle. He'd have had a happier life with Helene and maybe a family."

My phone rings and when I answer it, Paul informs me that Detective Gerard is on the line.

"I'm sorry," I say to Claude, "But I'll have to take this."

He stands, shakes my hand and obediently makes his way to the door. Before he leaves he turns and says, "There is one person you might want to check out, Danielle. Michelle had dealings with a man called Juan Gonzales. He's a nasty piece of work and a real slippery fish. He did several deals with Michelle, deals she kept very private. A lot of money was involved. I think he owns a house near Le Perthus, right on the border, and I believe he has business interests in Spain and in France."

I thank Claude, scribble down the name then turn my attention to the phone call.

"Sorry for keeping you, Sir," I say. "I was just finishing an interview."

"I just called to see if you've spoken to Jacques, yet?" he asks.

When I inform him that I have, he exhales his bated breath.

"And you've reached the same conclusion as me? Jacques didn't kill his wife."

I feel my skin prickle. "I don't know anything for sure yet," I reply. "I'm not able to draw any conclusions at the moment. I'm at a very early stage of the investigation. Of course, I'll keep you informed, Sir. Off the record, I don't think Jacques was involved."

"Good, good, that's all I wanted to hear. Keep up the good work and send me a report of your findings as soon as you can."

The phone clicks off and I'm left listening to the dial tone. I'm raging mad – how dare he? I think. He might be my boss, but he's not my keeper. Is he going to phone me every day? I stand and kick the wastepaper bin, sending its contents flying out in all directions. I need some answers fast or that interfering busybody is going to drive me around the bend.

Chapter 9

By late afternoon, we are thoroughly fed up dealing with stupid people. If another holidaymaker comes into the office with a ridiculous request or a tedious problem, we will all become stark, raving mad. Added to this, the heat has built up unbearably, it's in the high twenties and the air is oppressively heavy. By five o'clock, I find myself staring at the clock willing the minutes to tick by. Unable to stand any more of the stuffiness, I go outside to try and get some breaths of fresh air. As I glance towards the Canigou, the highest peak in the region, I see grey cloud rolling down the mountainside. The sky is blackening and I know we will soon have rain. I find myself welcoming the distant thunder and wonder if I'll be able to lock up and make it to my car before the storm breaks.

I return to my office and telephone Patricia to let her know the storm is on its way. She was planning to do a lot of washing today and I know if she's busy making preserves, she might not notice that it's going to rain. The washing will be dry by now and there's nothing worse than seeing all the effort of hanging it out going to waste then having the soaking mass draped around the house. When we have summer storms in this part of the world, it's like standing under a power shower. The rain cascades down, turning the road into a river and the river into a raging torrent. The best thing about it for us locals is that it drives the tourists into the bars, restaurants and shops and they spend more of their money. When I get through to her, she tells me that the washing is not only in the house, but ironed and put away as well.

"I'll just run out and get the chair covers," she says. "If it's going to rain, we'll have to dine indoors. I've invited Sarah to dinner. I hope you don't mind. We're going to discuss the stalls for the *festival taurin*, the bullfight weekend."

I find Sarah rather irritating. She's obsessed with animals and she always seems to have a distinct odour of cats clinging to her clothes. I'd much rather not dine with her, particularly as we're to be stuck inside, but Patricia is going to need her if I'm to get the day off from helping, so I say nothing derogatory.

I feel I should remain in the office until lock up time at six o'clock, but I send Laurent and Paul home early so they don't get soaked. Then I telephone Pascal Boutiere's office to arrange an appointment to see him. I want to find out exactly what he and Michelle have been up to regarding the withheld deposits and any dodgy deals. I want to know if any of them might have led someone to murder. When I make the call, I'm put through right away.

"Bonjour, Danielle, I was expecting your call," he says. "Actually, I'm rather relieved. I've been worried for quite some time, you see."

"I'd like to meet up and talk to you about Michelle," I reply. "When can we get together?"

"Any time; the sooner the better, I can clear any business out of the way. Just let me know a time and I'll come to the office, shall I?"

"I'd prefer to come to your office, if that's okay," I reply. "We're less likely to be overheard. How about ten tomorrow morning?" I've suggested this so I can have access to any files he may have that are relevant.

"Yes, ten's fine, thank you. *A demain*, until tomorrow."

Once I've got the information from Pascal, I'll know the questions to ask Marie Ribes. Being Michelle's secretary, she should have access to all manner of interesting and potentially damaging facts.

The heavens open just as I'm locking the door and the short dash to my car leaves me dripping wet and bedraggled. At least once I'm home, I needn't go out again as Sarah has her own transport, so I won't be expected to chauffeur her. I reach the house in less than ten minutes and the delicious smell of Patricia's cooking welcomes me as soon as I open the door. Sarah is already there and both girls step forward to help me out of my wet jacket. Ollee is gnawing on a meaty bone and barely lifts his head from his task, although his tail drums the floor.

While we are seated at the table I make a mental note never to leave Sarah and Patricia alone for very long as Sarah imparts one tear-jerking story after another, mostly about cats, but with the odd dog thrown in for good measure. When she starts to produce photos from her handbag, of cute abandoned kittens and puppies, I know where this conversation is going. Patricia's heart is melting with every tale of woe. Her eyes have taken on a glazed, soppy look and I know I must step in and nip this in the bud before we find ourselves re-homing half the stray cats in town. I'm forceful, almost to the point of rudeness, when I cut into yet another heart-wrenching story and endeavour to change the subject away from anything furry or fluffy.

"You're a friend of Marie Ribes, aren't you?" I ask Sarah. "What's she like?"

Sarah pauses and drops her second bundle of snapshots featuring a three-legged dog and a maimed, one-eared cat back into her handbag. I have her full attention. We are saved.

"Marie and her husband Franck are absolute saints," she begins. "They've adopted three cats and two dogs over the last two years. As soon as they moved from their apartment into a house, they've cared for needy animals and offered them a home."

"Very commendable," I agree. "I'm surprised they can afford a house. I didn't think Michelle Moliner would pay her secretary very much and I'm sure Franck doesn't fare much better working as an odd job man and part-time gardener."

"They don't have any children draining what resources they do have," Sarah says. "Marie told me Michelle never employed people with children. She wanted their full attention when they were working for her, without distractions. But with regard to Marie's earnings – as well as being the secretary in the office, she worked as a personal assistant for Michelle, helping her with her other business, and that was very well paid."

Sarah has my full attention. "What other business would that be?" I ask. My heart is pounding in my chest with anticipation.

"I'm not exactly sure. But Marie told me it's something to do with buying and selling property using large sums of cash. She said there were always lucrative cash deals to be made and these transactions were negotiated without using the *notaire* until the final exchange of contracts. I don't know all the ins and outs of it, but Marie often invited me out to celebrate with her when such a transaction was completed. On these occasions, she always picked up the bill. She is very kind and generous."

"I take it she also adopted an animal at each of these get-togethers," I say.

"Oh, yes, that's right. We've been out five times in the last two years and Marie and Franck now have five pets. As I said, she is very kind and generous."

And very soft and stupid, I think. I throw a knowing look in Patricia's direction and she returns a wry smile to me. Then her face lights up and her blue eyes sparkle and she begins to laugh softly.

"It's just as well there will be no more of these special transactions now that Michelle is gone, or Marie and Franck would need to buy a bigger house."

By ten o'clock, the full force of the storm has passed and we have managed to avoid adopting one of Sarah's sob stories. I can't wait to interview Marie Ribes and ask her about her role in the 'special transactions' and what sort of money changed hands. The evening has ended up so much more interesting and useful than I ever imagined it would.

When we are showing Sarah out I grab an umbrella from the stand at the front door and escort her to her car.

"You don't think Marie or Franck had anything to do with Madame Moliner's death, do you?" Sarah asks as we walk down the path.

"No, absolutely not," I say and I can see a look of relief pass over her face.

"Marie and I are very close friends," she explains. "I wouldn't want her to think I was speaking out of turn."

"You have said nothing wrong and I'm sure Marie has done nothing to harm Michelle," I reassure her.

Sarah climbs into her car and I watch as she drives off. No, Marie has not harmed Michelle, I think. Michelle has managed to cause harm all by herself with her dodgy business deals, and one of those dodgy deals might very well have cost her her life.

Chapter 10

I take my time getting ready in the morning and leave the boys to open the office. My meeting with Pascal Boutiere is at ten and I plan to make that my first work of the day.

"Marjorie is driving me to Perpignan this morning. Is there anything you need there?" Patricia asks as I pour myself an extra cup of coffee. "I've sold a couple of paintings," she explains. "There's cash waiting for me at the gallery."

"I don't need anything in Perpignan, but my Papa could use a new work shirt. He managed to catch the sleeve of one of his when he was pruning trees in the orchard last time, and he's never replaced it. I hate seeing him wearing that old thing with its elbow ripped. If you could pick up a couple of new ones, I'd be most grateful. The shop is quite close to the gallery."

"Of course, Danielle, it'll be no bother at all. I'll buy your mama a pretty scarf while I'm at it, then she won't feel left out. Perhaps I should invite them to come for dinner tomorrow evening."

"Thanks, Patricia, but I think dinner is a step too far. I'm right in the middle of an investigation and I don't think I could deal with my mother. I know she's mellowed a bit, but she's still a very difficult woman." My mother and I have never got on very well. "Why don't you invite Papa for lunch?" I suggest. "And I'll try to drop in to see him. Then we can give him his gift without having to spend time with my mother."

Patricia purses her lips. She believes in building bridges and she always tries to please my mother, even though she knows the woman is a bigot who judges her unfairly.

"Well, if you're sure you can't do dinner, I'll organise lunch tomorrow, say about one o'clock?"

"Fine, yes, I'm sure I can make that," I reply.

From suggesting one generous gesture, I'm now feeling slightly uncomfortable, as if I've done something wrong or been found to be lacking. My mother always makes me feel inadequate even when she's not present. I guess I'll never truly have her approval and I wonder why, after all this time, I still seek it.

* * *

Pascal Boutiere's office is modern and minimalist in style. It's recently been renovated and I suspect the simple furniture and décor has cost a fortune. I guess our young *notaire's* business is doing rather well. When he comes out of his office into the general area to greet me, he sees me running my hand across the coffee table top approvingly, touching the moulded smoothness of it. It is very tactile.

"I really like what you've done with the place," I say. "Business must be good," I add.

Pascal blushes. "Oh, you know how it is. The public expects a certain standard."

"Still, this is expensive kit," I reply. I don't know why, but I'm like a dog gnawing on a bone and just won't let it go. "You must have some very wealthy clients."

Pascal hangs his head for a moment. He looks uncomfortable, as if he doesn't know how to move on.

"Will you want some coffee?" the receptionist offers, breaking the silence.

"Yes, yes, in my office please, Collette." He breathes a sigh of relief. "This way, Danielle," he says and I follow as he leads me down a narrow corridor.

We sit at opposite sides of an elegant desk. Pascal seems rather nervous. He's usually calm to the point of being boring, but not today. He is fidgety and twitchy and is wringing his hands. After a minute or two of sitting in silence watching his discomfort, the door is opened and Collette brings in the coffees.

"Can I get you anything else?" she asks.

"No, thank you, Collette, just shut the door when you leave, please," Pascal replies.

She throws me a slightly worried glance, which I find unusual, then leaves us alone.

Pascal takes a couple of gulps of the scalding coffee then says, "I'm not sure where to begin. I'm not sure what you want to know."

"You said you were expecting my call and you wished to tell me something. You are obviously troubled and it has something to do with Michelle's death, so why don't you start by telling me what you're afraid of. Has Michelle upset someone who could be dangerous?"

He exhales his bated breath, stands and paces the room like a trapped animal. "Michelle has upset lots of people. I tried to warn her. I told her that although some of her dealings weren't technically illegal, they were morally suspect and might be challenged in court. But she just laughed it off. Now she's dead and I'm terrified of being implicated. What if the killer focuses on me? I had no part in any of these controversial transactions, but I was her chosen *notaire* on other deals. People might think I'm somehow connected, even though I'm innocent."

The use of the word 'innocent' in this way makes me think that Pascal sees Michelle as having been guilty of something.

"I think this would be the time to tell me what's been going on, don't you? I can't advise you whether you're at risk until I know what's involved. When news of Michelle's death spread around town, people congregated at my office and one woman, Madame Bergere, mentioned being worried about a deposit Michelle was holding for her. Was this one of those controversial transactions?"

"No, no, not at all, Madame Bergere's money is in the bank. I lodged it there myself. No, the money in question has all come from foreigners. Two English men and one Irishman have appointed a solicitor and are awaiting a court date, but as I said before, the transactions weren't actually illegal." He stops talking to gulp down more coffee, draining the cup. Then he sits back down on his chair, places his elbows on the desk and holds his head in his hands. He doesn't look up, instead his shoulders begin to heave and I realise he's crying, so I wait in silence until he can compose himself once again. After a couple of minutes, he mops his eyes with a tissue and begins again.

"I knew what Michelle was doing, but I wasn't involved and I didn't approve. You must believe that. I didn't approve of any of it, but she was blackmailing me, you see. As you rightfully pointed out, all this doesn't come cheaply." He sweeps his hand in front of him to encompass the room. "Michelle provided the money for the renovation and in return, I let her use my offices for her business deals. Doing the transactions in a *notaire's* office made them seem legitimate, even though there was no paperwork to back them up."

Pascal reaches into his desk drawer and extracts a bottle of brandy and two glasses. "Will you have some?" he offers.

"It's a bit early in the day for me," I reply. "But don't let me stop you."

He pours himself a hefty measure then returns the bottle and spare glass to the drawer and I wonder how often he knocks back alcohol this early in the day. I hadn't noticed before, but now, as he raises the glass to his lips, I see his hand has the distinctive shake of a heavy drinker. Pascal sighs and rubs his forehead with his fingertips, as if trying to ease a pain. Then he begins to speak again.

"The two Englishmen are friends, so they appointed the same solicitor to act for them. Quite by chance, they met the Irishman at his office, so now all three are in contact with each other. They have each paid over twenty thousand euros and have got very little in return."

My memory is stirred back to my earliest case, when Monsieur Stephen Gold fell to his death from a building in the centre of town and I mention it to Pascal. An English couple were involved in a shady deal with him where he tried to retain their deposit, claiming it was just his fee for services.

"Yes, yes, that's exactly what's happened here," Pascal agrees. "Michelle took their deposit money for a purchase of property, the deal fell through, but she kept their cash. No paperwork had been completed apart from her contract and her contract gave her the right to claim up to ten per cent of the purchase price as fees. So you see, the paperwork is legal, but as I said before, morally wrong. She claimed she had a right to her fee as she'd found them the property to buy, thus completing her part of the bargain. They maintain that they only handed over the money as a deposit for the said property, and as the deal fell through, the money should be returned to them. It's a horrible mess and I have no idea what will happen when it goes to court."

"But surely these men would have an interest in Michelle staying alive? You can't sue a dead woman."

"No, that's true, but you can sue her beneficiary. Although you're right, I can't see any of them being angry enough to kill Michelle. They don't want to be cheated out of their money, but they are all very wealthy men, and besides, none of them are in town. They all live overseas."

"I've heard mention of the occasional special transaction where large sums of money change hands. Do you know anything about that?" I ask. I'm trying to draw the name 'Juan Gonzales' out of him.

Pascal pales. He gulps down more brandy then reaches into his desk drawer, lifts the bottle and tops up the glass. "I'm not sure what you mean. Which transactions are you referring to? What have you heard?"

"I think you know exactly what I've heard, Pascal, so why don't you stop all this nonsense and tell me what's been going on. I can't protect you if you don't provide me with the information."

Pascal stares hard into my eyes, as if trying to decide what to tell me. Then he says, "I'm scared, Danielle, I'm really terrified. Michelle has been doing business with a Spaniard called Juan Gonzales. Have you heard of him? He's a loan shark. Very nasty, very dangerous. She's been helping him to launder money. That's all I know, she didn't involve me at all."

"Why would he want to harm her? Surely keeping her well and nurturing their friendship was tantamount to his business surviving."

Pascal gets up and paces the room again. "She was cheating him, Danielle. Over the past few months she'd skimmed off over fifty thousand euros. She gloated about it to me. She said Gonzales was an idiot who'd left school at fourteen and couldn't count to save himself."

"And do you think that was true?" I ask. "Or do you think she was just showing off to you?"

"No, it was true all right. She had his money and Gonzales knew it. I'm really scared, Danielle. He came here to talk to me a couple of weeks ago. He looked around the office and said that he could see where his money had gone and if Michelle didn't return his cash, he'd know exactly where to come to get it back. He put his hands on me, Danielle, he grabbed my lapel. What will I do if he returns? I don't have his money and I don't know where it is."

Oh, merde, I think. What a mess. Now I have a potential suspect who's capable of murder. "Is this man Gonzales upset with anyone else, or just you? Is he likely to threaten anyone else?"

"Perhaps Monsieur Claude," Pascal says. "On one occasion, the four of us had lunch together and Michelle introduced Claude to Gonzales as a business associate. I don't think he knows anyone else. He never stayed in town overnight. He just came in to do the transactions then left the same day."

"And you have absolutely no idea where his money is? No hidden bank accounts or safety deposit boxes?"

"Believe me, Danielle, if I knew where his money was I'd give it all back to him. I don't even know how to get in touch with him. I've been sitting here every day, terrified that he's going to come through that door and hurt me. I'm a nervous wreck. I can't function."

"I can understand your fear, Pascal," I reply. "I don't know what to suggest, because if I can't contact the man, I can't interview him or warn him off. Until he comes back here there's not a lot I can do. I certainly can't pursue him in Spain. All I can suggest is that if you do see him in town, call me immediately." I hand Pascal my card with my mobile number, but I hope he never calls.

"But what if he barges in here and threatens me – or worse, hurts me? What if he grabs me off the street or comes to my home?"

"I'm sorry Pascal, but I don't know what to tell you. My hands are tied. Perhaps you should contact Patricia's friend, Sarah and get a dog; the bigger the better."

"Knowing my luck, Gonzales will shoot me and the dog," he replies miserably. "Then a poor, innocent creature will be condemned to die as well."

Chapter 11

I take a leisurely stroll towards the main street so I can walk past Molliner's estate agency. It's nearly lunchtime, but I hope to find Marie Ribes in the office. The sooner she and I can have a little chat, the better. The day is sunny, very hot and the town centre is busy. Tourists and 'curists', who are clients of Monsieur Claude's spa, are popping up like a heat rash on pale skin. Most of the outside tables at the bars and cafes are full. A colourful mixture of shorts and T-shirts, sun hats and visors, towels and sunglasses adorn tables, chairs and the floor. Hot, fractious children accompany the red-faced adults who are loudly and rudely attempting to get service from overworked waiters, and with the irritating buzz of their dissatisfaction assaulting my ears, I remember all the reasons why I dislike having to be here during July and August. My town has been invaded and if it wasn't for the money these demanding, bad-mannered people bring, I'd happily close all doors to them.

A small crowd has formed around a table outside a café. Their faces are strained with concern, and as I push my way nearer to see what's going on, I hear Doctor Poullet's distinctive grumbling and notice his car illegally parked, at a crazy angle on the double yellow lines.

"Of course he is unconscious, you stupid woman! He's lain in the sun all morning then drunk himself into a stupor. Have you English never heard of the word 'decorum'?"

A plump, middle-aged woman in tomato-coloured shorts and blouse is weeping softly. Her eyes match the colour of her clothes. Cedric, the proprietor, is trying to usher people back to their seats. His face is wet with perspiration and dark patches are forming on his shirt at the armpits and down the middle of his back.

"Nothing to see here," he says. "Please, either go back to your seats or pay your bill and leave. Give the poor man some air."

"Yes, and give this poor man some space," Poullet says, talking about himself. "Go on, be off with you," he barks, as he shoves people unceremoniously out of the way. "Ah, Danielle," he says when he spies me. "At last, some assistance from the police. Not before time."

I'm about to protest that I've received no call for help, but realise it is futile. So instead, I endeavour to disperse the crowd. It's only when the gathering moves on that I realise the unfortunate couple's friends are still sitting at a nearby table, supping vast quantities of local wine, oblivious to or uncaring about their friend's position. They glance over between gulps to give a 'thumbs up' signal to the wife, but that is the extent of their support.

"This man must go to hospital. He is seriously dehydrated," Poullet says. "*Avez vous* insurance?" he asks the hapless wife. She stares at him blankly. "Have you insurance? INSURANCE?" he shouts, spelling out the word in English. "Or perhaps a credit card? CREDIT CARD?"

She sobs loudly. "I don't have anything with me! We're staying in Céret. Everything is in our apartment. What will I do? What can I do? Please don't let Billy die."

Poullet slaps his forehead with frustration. "Madame, your husband is not going to die. Do something, Danielle. Do something before I have a mental breakdown," he says, turning to me. "The man is in the recovery position. I've done all I can for him. I'm leaving now to meet Monsieur Claude for lunch. This is now a job for the police." Poullet grasps a chair and uses it to struggle to his feet, while I telephone for an ambulance.

"I suggest you see if your friends have a credit card with them," I tell the wife. "You're going to need some way of paying the ambulance and the clinic."

She scurries over to them and within a couple of minutes, she returns triumphant. "My friend Charlie will go in the ambulance," she says. "He's got a credit card."

"At the rate the friend has been drinking, he might require assistance from the clinic as well," Poullet observes. "Between them, they have no more brains than a rocking horse. I'll be so glad when the season is over and the foreigners go back to Stupidland, or wherever else these idiots call home."

Cedric stands beside me for a chat as we await the arrival of the ambulance. His waiters resume serving customers. The man on the ground is ignored, the moment has passed and the excitement is over.

"It was lucky I saw Poullet driving down the street when the man collapsed," Cedric says. "But when I stepped off the pavement to flag him down, the silly old fool nearly ran me over. His driving is atrocious and it's getting worse."

I nod in agreement and we watch as Poullet waddles towards his car. The lady dressed in tomato red pursues him. "You can't just leave my husband lying in the street!" she says. "You'll have to wait for the ambulance, surely? What if he deteriorates?" She grabs at Poullet's arm.

"Unhand me, Madame. It is not my fault your husband drank himself into oblivion. I helped you out of the goodness of my heart and to assist the *patron*, my good friend Cedric. Your husband is not my patient and nor do I wish him to be. If you require a doctor to hold your hand until the ambulance arrives, I suggest you ask the police to summon one." He pulls his arm free and resumes walking towards his car.

"You call yourself a doctor!" the woman cries. "You don't care one hoot for human life. How can you just walk away?"

Poullet does not turn around, he simply shrugs, opens his car door and climbs inside. Winding down the window, he calls out. "Like this, *Madame*, I walk away on my two good legs, like this." Then he starts the engine, turns the steering wheel and drives off in a cloud of exhaust fumes, clipping an ornamental plant pot at the side of the pavement as he goes. The woman throws up her arms with exasperation, while Cedric and I try to stifle our chuckles.

"Some things will never change," Cedric says. "We will always have English peasants drinking themselves unconscious and Poullet will always be a bad-tempered, cantankerous old devil."

"Ah, but he is a very good doctor," I reply. "And you know what they say; better the devil you know."

The minutes' tick by as I await the arrival of the ambulance. When I glance at my watch, I realise that unless I leave immediately, Moliner's office will be closed for lunch before I get there.

"Have you somewhere to be?" Cedric asks. "Don't worry, I can see this man into the ambulance and on his way – I'm sure they'll be here soon."

"Thanks Cedric, but I'd better wait. I don't want these drunks turning nasty."

I consider calling the office to get one of my assistants to relieve me, but even if they left right away, it's doubtful I'd make it to Moliner's in time. Instead, I decide to make the best of a frustrating situation so I sit at a nearby table and order a chicken salad and an ice-cold beer.

"How can you eat when my husband is lying ill at your feet?" his wife asks. She holds her open hands in front of her and raises her eyebrows at me. By the disapproving look on her face, it seems she thinks I'm doing something wrong.

"Don't worry, Madame," I reply, mildly annoyed. "He is not upsetting my meal any more than he is disturbing your friends' drinking."

Chapter 12

The ambulance duly arrives and within minutes, removes its charge to the hospital. The remainder of their party follow in a hastily-summoned taxi. Calmness returns and I take my time finishing my lunch for which I am not charged.

"It's on the house, Danielle. Thank you for all your help. I'm sorry you missed your appointment," Cedric says.

I did little to deserve a free lunch, but I'm not complaining. When I leave the café, I walk past the estate agency only to see a sign on the door informing me it will be closed until Thursday, owing to bereavement. I've wasted my time coming here, and decide I'll have to try and contact Marie and Franck Ribes at their home.

When I get back to my office I telephone the Ribes land line number, but there is no reply. The only other number I have is for Franck's mobile. It rings out eight times and I'm just about to hang up when a gruff voice says, "Henri, I've told you it's difficult for me to answer the phone now, I'm digging a pit for a septic tank and I'm up to my neck in a hole. What do you want this time?"

"Monsieur Ribes, I'm sorry, I am not Henri. It's Danielle, from the police. I need to speak to you and your wife about Michelle Moliner."

"Danielle! Oh yes, sorry, I'm having a difficult day. Sincere apologies, but Marie is in Gerona today visiting her friend. I'm nearly finished my work here, another two hours should see it through then I'll be working at the field adjacent to your father's orchard, Madame Ancel's kitchen garden to be exact. If you'd like to meet me there, say at about four, I'd be delighted to answer any questions you might have. Anything I can do to help."

I don't correct Franck by explaining the orchard belongs to Patricia. She would happily give my father the kudos of being the owner; besides he does most of the work there.

"Four will be fine," I reply. "Until then."

I spend my time completing a crossword and drinking coffee as the minutes' tick away. I can't get enthusiastic about the paperwork that has been piling up on my desk, so I hand it over to be dealt with by Laurent. Although his work is slow and he's a bit of a dolt, he does have a marvellous knack of coping with tedious jobs like recording information and filing. At first, Paul laughs about Laurent being landed with the job, thinking he is being let off the hook. That is until the inevitable procession of time wasters come through the door in a steady stream, and he has to deal with them himself as Laurent is already fully occupied. From time to time I can hear Paul's voice rising with frustration, followed by laughter from his colleague.

At three-thirty, I stand and gather up my bag, together with a couple of bottles of Perrier from my little fridge, tell the boys I won't be back, and practically skip out of the door into the sunshine. Then I quickly nip around the corner to the *boulangerie* and buy a couple of almond croissants to take with me to my meeting with Franck. We might as well relax in the sun for a few minutes while we talk, I think. Before I drive off, I telephone Patricia to let her know I'll be home early and she's delighted.

"I've got lots to tell you," she says excitedly. "But it can wait, it's nothing important."

Patricia usually has something exciting to tell me – exciting to her that is. Not necessarily exciting to me, but I can't wait to get home and see her nevertheless.

The drive to the orchard takes me only ten minutes and when I park at the gate, I can see Franck working in the adjacent field. He seems to be constructing a low, electric fence, presumably in preparation for the autumn and the onslaught of thieving wild boar. These greedy animals have broken the hearts of many farmers as they can strip a field or do irreparable damage in a few hours. By the look of Madame Ancel's garden, I expect most of the fruit and vegetables she relies on for food are grown here, and the electric fence will be a small price to pay to safeguard it.

When Franck sees me approach, he wipes his hand on a rag and comes to greet me.

"Bonjour Danielle, *ça va?*" he says.

"*Oui, tres bien, merci. Ça va, et vous?*" I reply.

"Yes, yes, I am good," he says. "And your father, he is well?"

"Yes, yes, very well, thank you. I thought he might be here today. He can't seem to stay away from the orchard."

"I've driven past many times and seen him working, he is very skilled with the trees. He seems to be really enjoying his retirement," Franck says. "Not that he's getting much rest. Looking after an orchard is a full-time job," he adds.

With the formalities of small talk taken care of, I show Franck my bag of croissants and the bottles of water. "Is there somewhere we can sit for a few minutes? Can you take a little break?"

"Yes, I'm getting tired and the heat's becoming too oppressive to work, so a break would be good. I have two tool boxes under that tree. We can sit on them in the shade." He points to a large sweet chestnut, growing at the edge of the field.

We make our way over the land, walking between the neatly arranged vegetable plots. When we are seated with our snacks Franck says, "Terrible business about Madame Moliner. I work for Jacques and he's a very fair man. I know her sister Helene as well. She's a real lady, very sweet and gentle. It must have been such a shock for them."

I notice that Franck calls Michelle, 'Madame Moliner', but speaks about Jacques and Helene using their first names. That tells me rather a lot about how he feels about them.

Franck Ribes is a patient, gentle man. I have never seen him flustered. He is the sort of person who inspires confidence. If ever someone has a problem that needs solving, Franck is the man to call. He can turn his hand to most things, be it gardening, bricklaying, painting, a cat stuck up a tree or a car that won't start in the morning – then Franck's your man. He is tall and broad with a flat, moon face. He's not conventionally handsome, but he has even features and a pleasant smile. We slip easily into conversation without being burdened by formality and I prefer it that way.

"When were you last at the Moliner house," I ask, turning the conversation to the questions I need answered.

Franck thinks for a moment. "Thursday, just last week, I was there doing a tidy up in the morning. Not for long, just a couple of hours, a bit of trimming and dead-heading roses, things like that. The ground was too dry and hard for much else. The sunshine and lack of rain makes it go like concrete."

"Was Madame Moliner at home when you were there?"

"They were all there; Madame Moliner, Jacques and Helene. Madame Moliner arrived to pick up some papers she'd forgotten. I was helping Helene to get a large paella pan out of the shed. It's enormous and very heavy, and she couldn't move it on her own. She told me she was lending it to a friend who's is cooking for the Céret *feria* on Saturday. She wanted to move it from the shed to the garage, so her friend could pick it up without disturbing the household. We had manoeuvred it into the garden when Madame Moliner came out to see what was going on. She blew up, shouting at poor Helene, telling her not to lend her things without first asking her permission. It was a ridiculous way to behave. The paella pan is only used a couple of times a year. If she hadn't seen me moving it, she probably wouldn't have known it was there. I'm sure it belongs to Jacques, anyway. Her outburst was very embarrassing. Helene's eyes filled with tears, she didn't know what to say. I walked away and busied myself at the other end of the garden."

"That must have been most uncomfortable for you," I agree. "What happened next?"

"Madame Moliner stormed off, I moved the paella pan to the garage, then I put away the things I'd taken from the shed to give access to the pan and I locked up. Helene kept apologising for her sister's bad temper. Helene is sugar and Madame Moliner was vinegar. I'm sorry she was murdered, but she'd upset so many people. Everyone disliked her and it was only a matter of time before she pushed someone beyond their limit."

We sit in quiet contemplation for a few minutes then Franck says, "I still can't understand how she came to die in the sauna. I've been told the door was locked, but that's impossible, there is no lock on the door."

I explain about the forked stick wedging the door closed.

"Oh, mon Dieu! Oh, no, I think I helped the murderer," Franck says. He holds his head in his hands.

"What do you mean? What did you do, Franck?"

"The forked stick, I took it out of the shed so I could reach the paella pan. I had to remove all manner of things, but I was so upset by Madame Moliner's behaviour, I threw the stuff back in hastily and locked the door when I was finished. I might have left the stick propped up against the shed. I can't remember. Its partner was on a rack on the wall, so I didn't have to move it."

"It's partner?" I repeat. "What are they used for Franck? The forensic expert said it was covered in animal fat residue."

"Yes, yes, that's right. They're the props for a spit. They support the metal rod which goes through the animal so it may be cooked over the fire. They're used at every barbecue. Metal sleeves are hammered into the ground next to a burning pit, then the props are pushed into the sleeves and the metal spit is suspended between them. I probably left it leaning against the side of the shed. I remember removing it, but I don't remember putting it back."

Of course, I think – that makes perfect sense, and if it was left in the garden, anyone could have had access to it.

"It's not your fault, Franck. The person who murdered Madame Moliner is to blame for her death. If they hadn't used the stick, they'd have found another way to kill her. Someone wanted her dead, and from my experience, when someone has a mind to kill, nothing will stop them."

Franck looks very upset. My words have done little to ease his feelings of guilt. I'm sorry for the man, but his action most likely did provide an opportunity for the killer. Perhaps if the stick had not been so readily available, Michelle might still be alive today.

Chapter 13

I wake in the morning with a slight headache, a dull thumping where the back of my head joins my neck. Although I slept without stirring my body feels heavy and I am still tired and lethargic. I feel as if I'm walking through thick soup and my cool shower does nothing to alleviate this. Patricia's exciting news of last night was something about my father and beekeeping, but I was only half listening. I suppose I'll get the whole story when I see him at lunch time. At my suggestion, Patricia has invited him to dine and I'm expected to attend, but the way I feel, I could do without the added pressure. I love my Papa and I enjoy spending time with him, but I've now received all the official documentation regarding Michelle's death and I must prepare my preliminary report for Detective Gerard before he comes looking for it.

I go through my usual routine, eat breakfast, drink coffee, small talk with Patricia, play with Ollee then I leave the house to begin my working day. The sky is grey and cloudy, the air oppressively heavy, the dull thump in my head increases and I feel like climbing back into my bed and skipping the day completely. If only I had the choice. I drive to work on automatic pilot and when I arrive at the office, I am greeted by Madame Bergere and her son, Denis, who are waiting patiently to speak to someone.

"Bonjour, Madame, Monsieur," I say. "What can I do for you today?" I try to keep my voice pleasant, but it's a struggle with the way I'm feeling.

"May we sit down, please? My mother finds it difficult to stand. Her arthritis is bad. It always flares up when she's upset," Denis replies.

"Of course, of course," I say, ushering them into my office and offering them seats in front of my desk. "I'm sorry, where are my manners? Please excuse me, I'm feeling rather tired this morning and the day has just begun."

They say all the right things, offering me sympathy and understanding before telling me the reason they are here.

"I'm worried about the money I paid to Madame Moliner," Madame Bergere begins. "I remember signing some paperwork, but I don't know what happened to it next. My son and I are moving from our family farm to a more manageable house here in town. My husband died last year and Denis has no interest in farming. I gave Madame Moliner the deposit money – twenty thousand euros."

"My uncle is taking on the farm, he has three sons, all farm workers," Denis explains.

Looking at Denis, I can see he'd never make a farmer. He has his mother's slight build, long elegant hands and his studious-looking grey eyes peer out from behind delicate, wire-rimmed spectacles. He looks more like an academic than someone who works with his hands. I don't understand why people always bring me their problems, when it's really nothing to do with the police, but in this instance, I can help to put Madame Bergere's mind at rest. She is a gentle, soft spoken lady and both she and her son have impeccable manners. It's refreshing compared to the moaning, bad-mannered tourists I've had to put up with recently.

"Madame, this is not really my field," I begin. "But I was speaking to the *notaire*, Monsieur Boutiere, the other day and I happened to mention your concerns. You were worried when you came to this office the day news of Madame Moliner's death was made public. He assured me that he had lodged your money in the bank. The paper you signed was the *compromis de vente* – you have nothing to worry about. I suggest you contact him."

Both she and her son are grinning at me, "Thank you, Officer, thank you so much, you've no idea how worried we were. That is such a load off our minds," Denis says.

"We've heard all these rumours about deposit money being lost. You're not sure what to believe," Madame says. "The day I was at the estate agency to hand over my deposit and sign papers, a Spanish man came into the office and he was very upset with Madame Moliner. He interrupted my meeting and he went on and on about some missing money. Madame's sister had to take over completing the paperwork with me, because Madame Moliner had to leave with the man half way through our appointment. I was a bit concerned, but the sister, Madame Lacroix, assured me everything was okay and the Spaniard's missing money had nothing to do with the agency. She is such a nice woman, she made me coffee and I believed her, but afterwards, when Madame Moliner was killed…" Her voice trails off.

"What did the man look like, Madame? Was he someone you recognised?"

"I didn't recognise him, but I would if I saw him again. He was very big and brutish with huge hands like a bear. He held them up as he spoke and I couldn't take my eyes of them. He towered over me as I sat on the chair and I found the whole experience rather intimidating. He just barged into the room, you see, uninvited. It was so rude of him. I was in the middle of my appointment. When Madame Moliner stood up to usher him out of the room, I could see he was twice her size, height and width. I wouldn't want to meet him on a dark lonely street; he frightened me."

"Is there a problem with this man?" Denis asks. "Do you think he had something to do with Madame Moliner's death? Could my mother be in any danger because she can recognise him?"

"No, no, nothing like that. I'm simply trying to match up some money that's been lodged with its rightful owners," I lie.

Madame Bergere lifts a package wrapped in baking paper from her bag. "Thank you for your time and all your help, Officer. This is something sweet for the staff to have with their coffee. I'm most grateful to you. Denis and I will go to Monsieur Boutiere today and sort things out."

We are given gifts like this quite often, but I'm touched that Madame Bergere brought this with her by way of thanks for my time. It's always nice to be appreciated. When I show them out of my office the phone begins to ring, heralding another busy day, but I leave Paul to answer it and ask Laurent to make me a coffee.

The morning passes quickly and before very long I'm on my way home for lunch. My thoughts are full of Juan Gonzales. From his description, he's not a man I would like to meet. However, I'm sure our paths will cross as he's not likely to give up trying to locate his money. The more I think about it, the more I realise that Michelle must have hidden it somewhere. It won't be anywhere conventional like a bank, but it must be a place she would have had easy access to. There must be a considerable sum hidden away and I would like to find it.

Chapter 14

When my father lost his job just a short time before he was due to retire, it was terribly stressful for him. He had always worked and was embarrassed to be seen during the day unemployed. The strain made him ill and I was worried sick that it would kill him. Fortunately, at that time, Patricia and I came into money and we bought our orchard. This enabled us to offer my father a lifeline by employing him to advise and assist us. We needed his help as we knew nothing about how to care for our trees, to get the most from them. He loved the work and we could pay him until he reached retirement age. It was a win, win situation. We would have continued to pay him a salary, but he flatly refused to accept our money, assuring us that his pension was more than adequate, and only agreeing to take a small amount of the produce for his and my mother's personal consumption.

Now we three are seated around the dining room table as Patricia serves lunch, and we both listen attentively to my Papa's new idea.

"Bees," he begins, "Honey bees, to be precise. For the past six months, I've been tending to bee hives owned by my friend, Monsieur Purcell. His health is bad and he and his wife are now moving to Paris to be close to their daughter. He has six hives and all the equipment for producing honey. His bees are strong and healthy. Because he needs to move quickly, and because we've been friends for many years, he's offered to give me the whole lot. He doesn't want any money from me, he just wants to know his beloved bees will be well cared for."

"Isn't it exciting, Danielle?" Patricia enthuses. "Your Papa will be a bee-keeper! He will have his own business producing and selling honey."

I want to be as enthusiastic as they are, but I'm actually a bit frightened of bees and I can't get my thoughts around encouraging them to share my space.

"Where will you place the bee hives?" I ask, hoping he doesn't say the walled garden. I couldn't stand having them there because I spend a lot of time in the garden tending to the rabbit hutches and the plants.

"The orchard," he says beaming. "It's the ideal location. I work there most days anyway and the bees will ensure the fruit trees are pollinated."

Now I am interested. I won't have to be exposed to the stinging creatures as I rarely spend time in the orchard.

"How much honey will six hives produce?" I ask.

"One hive could produce twenty-seven kilos in a good season. However, the average hive will have a surplus upwards of eleven kilos. They need about twelve kilos to survive the winter."

"That's a lot of honey," Patricia says. I can see by the look on her face she's already calculating the profit margin in her head.

"It's a perfect opportunity," Papa says. "My bees can pollinate your trees and your orchard and the surrounding farm land will feed my bees. I'm sure I'll be able to sell the honey at the local market."

"You won't have to," Patricia pipes up. "I'll take your whole production to complement my preserve and pickle business. I only need to make fifty cents profit a jar to cover the added work and you won't have to stand at a stall every week. I'll be benefiting by having a more reliable crop of fruit from my orchard."

"I won't make a fortune from the honey, but it will be very rewarding to produce something from my own business. I'll be able to tell people I'm a honey farmer and I'll join the beekeepers' association and attend conventions."

My Papa's excitement is palpable. I hadn't realised how important having a recognisable position is to him. He needs to feel productive, even though he is now past retirement age. It's nothing to do with the money. It's all about his pride.

He chatters on about bees, protective clothes, bee brushes, supers and all manner of kit until my eyes are glazing over. Patricia is rapt, her attention unwavering. I'm about to give an excuse to leave early and go back to work when my mobile rings. For a moment, I'm happy until I see the caller name displayed is Pascal Boutiere.

"Sorry," I say to Papa and Patricia. "But I have to answer this." They nod distractedly and keep talking about bees.

"Bonjour, Pascal," I say.

"He's here, Danielle. I saw him park his car and I ran and locked the outer door. Colette and I are hiding in my office. He's very angry, roaring like a mad bull. Can you hear that? He's banging on the glass door."

Even down the phone I can hear the thump, thump of something being banged. Pascal sounds frantic.

"Stay calm, I'm on my way," I say and I wave to Patricia and my Papa and run out of the door to my car.

"Don't hang up," Pascal begs. "Please, don't hang up. If he breaks in I want him to know the police can hear and you're on your way."

I begin to drive at breakneck speed. Fortunately, I now have a hands-free device for the phone so I can stay connected. When I'm only minutes away from the *notaire's* office, I can hear through the speaker, a terrible crashing sound and a woman, presumably Collette, screaming.

"Oh, mon Dieu, he's broken the outside door!" Pascal is now screaming too. "Go away! I'm on the phone to the police! They're almost here. Get out of here! They're arriving now."

Now I can hear another voice, a deep booming roar and further banging which I assume is the door to Pascal's private office then another crashing sound echoes over the hands-free speaker accompanied by more shouting.

The *notaire's* office is in sight, but I don't really want to tackle a brute of a man on my own, especially someone who can break through a security glass door.

"Hand him the phone, Pascal," I yell. "Put it on speaker. Let me talk to him."

Not knowing what's happening in the office I shout down the phone, "Whoever you are, this is the police. We are one minute from pulling up outside. There are several of us attending, so I suggest you leave the *notaire's* office immediately before you commit any further crimes. I know you're angry and we can talk about that, but I warn you now, if I find you on the premises, you will be going to jail." I keep talking, hoping Juan Gonzales hears me and responds. I'm hoping he's not beating up Pascal. "This is the police," I repeat. "We are parking now. Vacate the premises."

When I reach the car park, I see that Pascal's car is the only one there, parked in his designated space. Gonzales has obviously made a run for it, fearing the arrival of a squad of police officers. I begin to laugh, mostly from nerves. If only he knew that I am a small woman, all on my own. The heavy plate glass entranceway is smashed to pieces and so is the ornamental plant pot containing a small tree that used to stand to the side of it. I guess this is what Gonzales used to break down the door. I'm impressed – the man must indeed be enormous and very strong. I enter the building and gingerly walk down the narrow corridor towards Pascal's office. This door is also smashed. Pascal is sitting on his chair, crying. He has soiled his pants and a large wet patch reaches to his knees. Collette is slumped on the floor and she too, is weeping. I phone for back up and for the paramedics.

"I thought he was going to kill me," Pascal says. "He said if I didn't find his money he would hurt me. I'm sorry, so sorry, I've wet myself. I thought I was going to die." Pascal lifts his briefcase from the floor to cover his embarrassment.

"He ran when he heard your voice," Collette says. "He ran when he thought you were arriving. You saved our lives, Officer. I was standing in front of Mettre Boutiere and the brute threw me to the floor. I think he would have killed us. I really think we would be dead but for your swift actions."

I notice from what I've been told that Pascal was standing behind Collette. What a coward, I think, using a defenceless woman ās a shield.

"And the man who broke in, was it indeed Juan Gonzales?"

"Yes, it was him. Can you arrest him now? He broke into my office and assaulted Collette. Surely you can pick him up now?"

"Once you make your statements I'll have all the evidence I need, but first I must find him," I reply.

I suspect Gonzales is the sort of man who can appear and disappear at the drop of a hat and I'm not sure what to do if I do locate him.

Chapter 15

As is the way in a small town, news of Pascal's ordeal spreads like wildfire and by the time it returns to me, in the form of a telephone call from Jacques Moliner, it has grown out of all proportion.

"Helene and Marie Ribes are planning to open Michelle's office at noon today," he says. "I'm worried that they won't be safe. What if that madman Gonzales gets it into his head that they know something about his so-called missing money? I know they'll be just a few minutes from your office and right in the centre of town, but what could they do to defend themselves if this monster decides to smash up the place?"

I want to reassure Jacques but I don't know what to tell him. Michelle's office seems like the most likely next port of call for Gonzales.

"Jacques," I say. "Pascal locked the door when the man arrived. He refused to speak to him and Gonzales lost his temper. He's a hot head, but he didn't actually lay a finger on Pascal, and he simply pushed Collette aside. Not that I'm trying to defend his actions, but I do believe he's all noise and bluster, and now that he's had time to calm down, I imagine he'll lie low for a while."

I hear Jacques exhale. "So you think they'll be safe?" he asks.

"Yes, I'm quite sure nothing like this will happen again, but people do get upset when money is involved. You might want to consider doing something about the three outstanding court cases involving the English men and the Irishman, and Gonzales maintains he has given money to Michelle that is unaccounted for. I personally think he is telling the truth."

"The foreigners will have their money returned. Helene and I have already discussed this. She believes Michelle did nothing wrong, but we don't have the energy for a prolonged argument in court. As for the Spaniard, Helene knows nothing about his money, but she plans to discuss it with Marie today. If his money was being held by Michelle, then of course it will be returned."

I don't tell him that the cash most likely came from some illegal source, and if discovered, would be held by the authorities and possibly confiscated. Why upset him further? Instead, I advise him to inform Helene that I'll drop into her office at one o'clock when I'm on my lunch-time break, just to check all is well. It reassures him. I want to have a word with Marie in any case, and this kills two birds with one stone.

Saturday will soon be upon us and I'm aware that my car will not be big enough to carry Patricia's wares to the *feria* now that she'll be stocking two stalls, so I telephone a colleague in Céret who has a van, to arrange for his help. Patricia has already organised her stalls with her friend Elodie, who is a *savonierre*. Patricia stores the two stalls that she owns in Céret with Elodie and her husband Simon, and on the days she wants to use them, Simon delivers and constructs them for her in her allotted space. It's an arrangement that's been working well for several months now. Simon looks forward to receiving some of Patricia's produce in return for his work, and I don't have all the hassle of organising this part of her business.

Byron drops into the office bearing cake and has coffee with me while we discuss our arrangements for attending the bullfights. I explain to him that now Patricia has transport for her wares, Sarah will be driving us all through to Céret so he and I can have a drink or two.

"Or five or six," he quips.

"I've arranged parking for us," I say. "We'll just have to leave early enough to get into the space. Then the car will be stuck there until quite late at night. Patricia's friend, Elodie, has offered to give us a key to her home, in case any of us needs a rest through the day. In return, you and I can cover their stalls, if one of our friends needs to go to the toilet or have some food. It will be a very long day and probably rather exhausting, but enjoyable as well. The atmosphere at this event is amazing and attending the bullfights is like going back in time. They are full of ceremony and traditions."

"I've heard it can be a very drunken affair," Byron says. "One of my friends warned me not to dress in my best clothes, in case some drunk chucks up on me. Is that likely?"

"People do over-indulge," I agree. "It is *de rigueur*, but we'll just keep out of the way of anyone who is reeling or who has a green pallor. I suggest, if you have them, you wear the *feria* colours of red and white. Then we won't stand out from the crowd. The bullring, as you know, is just outside the centre of town, but it will be easy for us to get to it."

"How long will Patricia have to man her stall? Surely she won't be stuck there all day and evening?"

"Don't concern yourself, Byron. She and her friends will be selling their wares at the craft market, held for just a few hours on Saturday and again on Sunday, if she has any stock left. Then Simon will pack up her stall for her and he and Elodie will store any unsold goods until after the weekend, but don't worry, she'll sell everything, and probably on the first day."

"Just so long as she's not exposed to the drunken rabble, I can't bear to think of some disgusting sot peeing against her stall."

"Funny you should say that," I reply. "Some of the shop owners cover their shop fronts in polythene for just such an occurrence."

"Ugh!" is Byron's response and his face shows his disgust. "This is usually such a civilised part of the world. I guess critics of bullfighting are right, it really does bring out the worst in people."

We chat for a few minutes more, then when Byron is about to leave, I pick up my handbag and accompany him out of the door.

"I'm going to Michelle Moliner's office to have a talk with Marie," I explain.

"Good luck," he replies. "I'm going to go home to pour myself a gin and tonic, stuff a baguette with some fine ham for my lunch and read my paper sitting in the sunshine." With that said, he gives me a cheeky wink and we go our separate ways.

When I reach the estate agency, I can see through the glass shop front that the office is packed with people. Helene and Marie are both standing behind the counter, trying to deal with customers and they look harassed. I suppose closing the office during the busiest time of the year was not a good idea and they're suffering for that folly now. I know they'd planned to stay open every day, but I presume it just all got too much for them. Anyway, I think, there's no point in me trying to see either of them in that scene of bedlam. Instead, I quickly dart off in the direction of Byron's home. I guess he'll be having an unexpected guest for lunch.

* * *

I arrive back at Moliner's estate agency just as Marie is ushering the last customer of the day out of the door. When she sees me approach, she invites me in then turns the key in the lock to exclude any latecomers.

"What a horrible day," she says, as we make our way through to the rabbit warren of small offices at the back of the building.

Helene has her jacket on and she's preparing to leave for the evening. "Do you want to talk to me, Danielle?" she asks.

"No, thank you. I just want a couple of minutes of Marie's time then I'll be leaving. Don't wait behind on my account."

"Will you be okay, Marie? Do you mind if I go? I'll be with Jacques if you need me," she says.

Marie waves her hand dismissively. "You get along, Helene, and I'll see you tomorrow," she replies.

She offers me a seat in what was once Michelle's office, then slumps down into what was once Michelle's chair. Her thin face is strained and exhausted and her lips quiver, as if she may cry. She is a slightly built woman, but her steely grey eyes are hard and I'm sure in her household, she's the boss. I think her gentle lump of a husband will do exactly as he is told. I suppose her inner toughness is what allowed her to work closely with Michelle, without cracking up.

"Everyone who came into the office today had a problem. It's been very tiring, and as well as the disgruntled customers, behind the scenes, I've been trying to deal with lawyers and *notaires*. There just too much to do, in too little time. Lots of things that Michelle should have been dealing with, she's simply brushed aside. Helene is exhausted and now she's running home to look after Jacques as well. I don't know how she's coping with everything. On top of all this, we might now be at risk of a mad man coming here and smashing up the place." Now tears are flowing freely down her cheeks. "I'm sorry, but I'll have to telephone Franck and let him know you're here and I'm okay. Please excuse me for a moment."

She leaves the room to make her call and I stand and begin to look through the drawers of Michelle's desk. They are very untidy. A higgledy-piggledy mess of pens, screwed up bits of paper, chocolate bars – even a pair of tights – but nothing there of any significance. This is hopeless, I think to myself. How could anyone work like this? I sit back down and Marie re-enters the room.

"I'd like to discuss the special transactions," I say. "The deals that involved Juan Gonzales."

Marie's face flushes. "I don't know what I can tell you," she replies. "All I did was accompany Michelle to her meetings with the man. We always met at the *notaire's* office and each meeting was handled in the same way. Monsieur Gonzales gave Michelle a briefcase. I then left the meeting and took the case to the car while Michelle spoke to him. Then when Michelle came back to the car, she handed me an envelope to place inside the briefcase. I think I was there simply to be a back-up for Michelle and to remove the money and take care of it while she transacted the business."

"So the briefcase was full of money?"

"Oh, yes, thousands of euros."

"It all sounds rather clandestine to me."

"Yes, it felt that way to me," Marie admits. "I never understood what was going on, but Michelle was always happy to see Monsieur Gonzales and she was very generous with the overtime payment I received for helping her."

I bet she was, I think. I don't know what she was up to, but I'm sure the money involved came from an illegal source. I'm positive Michelle was helping the man to clean up dirty money.

"What happened to the money after Michelle returned to the car?"

"I don't know. After her meeting, she drove me home, handed me my extra pay in an envelope, then left. The briefcase remained in the car with Michelle." Marie's expression changes, and she looks worried. "Have I done something wrong? Have I broken the law in some way? I think now that Monsieur Gonzales might be a criminal."

"All you did was accompany your boss to a meeting. Gonzales might well be a criminal, but you had nothing to do with Michelle's arrangement."

Marie breathes a sigh of relief. "I've been so worried," she admits. "Michelle was always hopeless at paperwork. Helene and I are uncovering horrors with every file we open. It will take us weeks to sort out the mess, but at least now, I know I've done nothing wrong."

I feel I can't accomplish anything else here tonight so I stand to leave. "Are you ready to lock up now?" I ask.

"Yes, thank you. Let's get out of here. I've had more than enough for one day. There's just one thing, Danielle. What do I do if Monsieur Gonzales comes here looking for his money? I've no idea where it is, and there's no sign of it going into any of the bank accounts."

"Do you know how much money was involved?"

"Not exactly," she says. "But over all the transactions, there must have been upwards of a million euros. I know the last deal was for 200,000 euros."

I can't suppress a low whistle escaping from my lips. "If Gonzales comes anywhere near this office or anywhere near you, telephone me immediately and I'll deal with him. There was just one more thing, Marie. How soon after the last transaction was Michelle killed?"

She thinks for a moment. "Just a couple of days. Yes, we met in the *notaire's* office just a couple of days before her death."

"So, there's a chance she still had the case full of money?"

"I suppose so, but as I said before, I don't know what happened to any of the money. There is no sign of it being lodged anywhere. Do you think someone murdered her to get their hands on it?"

"I don't know why she was killed, but money is a strong motivator and nobody seems to know where it is."

Marie shudders. "I hope whoever killed Michelle realises that I don't have the cash. What if they come looking for me?"

These were precisely my thoughts.

Chapter 16

It's been a week since Michelle was murdered and I've interviewed everyone who had direct access to her home. I even have a suspect in the frame, but I think Juan Gonzales is unlikely to be her killer. He needed her; more importantly, he needed her alive. Particularly if he wanted to retrieve the money she'd stolen from him. I now don't believe that this attack was about money. Somebody had a grudge against Michelle. They wanted her to die in torment and there's a good chance they hung around long enough for her to see who locked her in. Once again this places her husband or her lover at the top of my list. I am certain this killing was a crime of passion. Detective Gerard is going to want answers – answers that don't involve his cousin, but I'm not sure how to proceed. My only choice is to keep trying to involve Gonzales. He's a criminal after all and he's probably guilty of something that he should be punished for.

I lie in bed pondering this dilemma for some time, but as it is Saturday and the day of the *feria* I must get a move on. I shower, dress in white jeans, a white blouse and top off my outfit with a red scarf tied at my throat, then I go downstairs where Patricia is waiting for Sarah and Byron to arrive. She looks beautiful, clothed in a pretty red and white dress with a red flower adorning her black hair. When she sees me, she immediately pours me a coffee.

"Sarah and Byron should arrive any minute," she says. "Sarah is picking Byron up so he doesn't have to use his car. She'll deliver us back here tonight, then she'll drive him home."

"Doesn't she mind not being able to have a drink?" I ask.

"No, she says she hardly touches alcohol because it's too fattening."

"Did Maurice get away with your stock okay? Did he manage to load it all into the van?"

"Yes, he and I managed very well and he was delighted with the painting I gave him as payment for his work. He's giving it to his Papa for his birthday next week. Did you know his father used to breed bulls?"

"No, I didn't," I reply. "How interesting; no wonder he was delighted with your painting."

We chat for another couple of minutes before Sarah and Byron arrive and we get on our way. Considering Byron said he was going to dress down for what will probably be a raucous occasion, he is, as usual, beautifully turned out in white linen trousers, a fine white linen shirt with a red sash at his waist and a red 'kerchief at his neck. Sarah is in a red skirt and white blouse.

"Well," she says. "Don't we all look grand in our *feria* colours?"

After checking we've forgotten nothing, we get on our way and before very long we arrive in Céret to the hustle and bustle of the celebrations. The girls stop to let us out of the car close to one of the bodegas, where some of my colleagues are already drinking.

"They'll be completely smashed by lunch time," Byron observes.

"Or possibly before," Patricia says. "Be careful you two don't get too intoxicated and don't try to run with the bulls."

"Spoil sport," Byron replies and Patricia wags her finger at him.

We watch them drive away before we go and order beer. We join in the fun, but manage to resist taking part in the running of the bulls, even avoiding the *vachettes*, the calves. After several hours and in a merry mood, Byron and I make our way with a crowd of others to the bullring. We choose *sombra* seating, the most expensive, in the shade. The day has become very hot, so we consider it money well spent. The sounds, smells and excitement of the bull fight are not for the faint-hearted and I see many tourists leave with sick expressions on their faces. Byron enjoys the atmosphere but admits that he too, is rather nauseated by the event.

"I cannot see the point in terrorising the poor beasts then killing them when they're exhausted and frantic. It's too cruel for me to find acceptable," he says. "However, the colours, costumes and ceremony are quite spectacular and I'm pleased you invited me to join you."

"So you won't be attending next year," I say.

"The *feria*, yes, but the bullfights, no. I'm afraid this will be my one and only visit to the bullring. It's a bit like fox hunting in England. I love the spectacle and the costumes. I even like seeing the pack of dogs leading the riders on horseback. If only they didn't run the poor fox to the point of exhaustion, then let the dogs rip it to shreds. I guess I'll never be a supporter of blood sports, I can't abide the cruelty."

I am sorry that Byron finds the bull fight cruel. I see it as a skilled sport, an art form like dance, which honours both the bull and the brave bullfighter. I suppose there are some differences between us and the English which will always remain. I salute my friend for his honesty and his acceptance that this is my tradition and he is the stranger in my country.

Chapter 17

I don't stir until late morning on Sunday, and when I do move myself, I find my whole mouth is like sandpaper and it's difficult to unglue my tongue from the roof of it. My body feels heavy and tired, but my spirits are uplifted. Yesterday was such a good day. As well as enjoying myself immensely at the *feria*, I have the added bonus of knowing Patricia and Sarah virtually sold out of all the stock. In fact, there were so few items left that we could carry them between us to Sarah's car and bring them home in the boot. Consequently, there was no requirement for Maurice and his van, and even better, Patricia will not need to man her stalls today.

I'm still in pyjamas and about to venture downstairs, when I hear voices. I can't be bothered getting dressed yet, so I strain to hear who is here and try to figure out if they are likely to be around for more than a couple of minutes. Ollee must have heard me moving because suddenly there is a drumming on the stairs, my door is pushed open and the dog leaps onto the bed, yapping.

"Shush, you idiot, shush," I say, putting my finger to my mouth, but it is of no avail. The mad little clown jumps off the bed and launches himself at me with his wet tongue and whacks my legs with his ridiculous tail. Now that I am fully awake, I can hear my Papa talking to Patricia, so I hastily wash, throw on a comfortable jogging suit and head downstairs. Ollee, who has waited outside the bathroom for me, overtakes me on the stairs and practically trips me up in his attempt to herald my arrival. We are all sitting at the table drinking coffee and eating croissants, while discussing the practicalities of moving the bee hives, when my mobile rings.

"Danielle, it's me, I need to talk to you. I don't want Patricia to hear us. I don't want to upset her."

It's Monsieur Claude and I've no idea what this is about, but he's said enough to stir my concern.

"I can go into the office in an hour's time, if you'd like, and I can meet you then," I reply without mentioning his name.

"That's great, Danielle, but why don't we meet at Cedric's café and I'll treat you to some lunch."

"Yes, that's fine, until then," I reply and cut off the call.

"Who was that? Surely you don't have to go into work today?" Patricia asks.

"No, I'm just going to retrieve a file I left at the Céret office. One of my colleagues is bringing it over for me. I'm not doing any work, but if you and Papa are spending time together making plans, I'll have some lunch in town with the man. I'll return in a couple of hours and be available to drive you home any time after that, Papa."

With the arrangements made, I have another cup of coffee, add my input to the conversation, and by the time I leave, I know more about moving bee hives than I ever wished to know.

When I arrive at the café, Claude is already there. We order some food and when the waiter leaves us I say, "What's this all about, Claude? Why would Patricia be upset?"

He sighs, rubbing his eyes with his hand, trying to find the right words.

"It's that criminal," he begins. "Juan Gonzales. He telephoned me. He's speaking to everyone Michelle knew. He accused me of being involved in some property scam, but I can promise you I know nothing about anything like that."

"Why would he think you were involved?"

"As I said, he's fishing – speaking to everyone. It's only a matter of time before he seeks out Patricia because she and I both own the building where Michelle rented a studio for her lover."

I'm worried sick. I don't want this dangerous madman anywhere near my beloved girl. "Have you any idea what Michelle was involved in?" I ask.

"I think I've managed to work it out," Claude replies. "I'm pretty sure Gonzales' money is dirty. He's a loan shark who handles vast sums of cash. I think Michelle was taking the cash and converting it into property, with every purchase being across the border in Spain and I think, for all his protestations, Pascal Boutiere knew exactly what was happening, but turned a blind eye because he wasn't directly linked to the transactions."

"Gonzales smashed up Pascal's office," I say. "Do you think he's a danger to you or Patricia?"

"I'm almost sure I convinced him we know nothing about any cash – as I said, he's on a fishing trip, but it probably won't stop him from seeking out Patricia to question her. I thought you should know. I'm pre-warning you so you can prepare Patricia in any way you think fit. The man is huge, by the way. He's an ugly monster of a human being. You might want a couple of strong young officers to accompany you if you decide to go and talk to him."

I'd rather not talk to Gonzales, but I can't let him approach Patricia, so I'll have to think of a plan. I cannot have this man threatening members of my community, but I'll have to be careful because physically, I'm no match for him and the strength of the law seems to hold no fear for him either.

Chapter 18

We are no sooner in the office on Monday morning, when we receive a call informing us that the Moliner estate agency has had a break in and requesting us to attend. Paul and I go around immediately. From outside the shop, there is no obvious sign of trouble, but when we enter, it's a different story. Every drawer, shelf and cupboard has been systematically emptied of its contents, which are strewn across the floor. Helene and Marie are both shocked and in tears. The front door is once again closed to the public, who are queuing up outside hoping to air their grievances and petty problems. Paul sends them on their way then places a notice in the window informing people that the office is closed. Amidst the chaos, when I glance out of the window, I'm certain I see Guy Legler hurry past on the other side of the street. I wonder what he's doing in town, but I cannot leave here now to speak to him.

"Who would do such a thing? How can we possibly sort this out?" Marie says, holding her hands in front of her in despair. "Michelle's files were in a mess before and we were only just beginning to make sense of things. Now there's no chance of getting on top of it and we have tourists and 'curists' arriving every day this week for their *locations*. I just hope they've all got the copies of their paperwork with them, or we won't even know which accommodation to put them in."

Helene straightens an overturned chair and sits down. She buries her head in her hands.

"This is all Michelle's fault," she says bitterly. "She brought all this trouble to the business with her greed and stupidity. Now we're faced with an impossible situation. We have unhappy clients queuing up at the door, a mess of paperwork at our feet and a criminal pursuing us. We don't know how to proceed, Jacques is depressed and I feel like putting a match to this place."

Marie dries her eyes and slowly begins to gather up papers from the floor. "Michelle was good to me," she states, regaining her composure. "She gave me a job when I needed one and she paid me well. I know she was your sister, Helene, and sisters always have differences, but she treated me fairly. If we clear this front part of the office, you can deal with the public while I try and sort out the mess. Only tackle the people who arrive for their *locations*, give them their keys and send everyone else away. From memory, there are four bookings due to arrive today and look, I've found the diary, so we'll know who they are and where they're going." She holds a large leather-bound book aloft. "I'll not be beaten by a thug. How dare someone do this, how dare they?"

Marie is showing incredible inner strength. Obediently, Helene removes Paul's hastily written sign from the window and positions herself at the front door, ready for the onslaught.

"He gained access by smashing through the back door," Paul states, having checked the premises. "I'll telephone the joiner now to come and secure it for you."

"Is there anything else we can do for you now?" I ask. "Are you sure you want to open up today? You've both had a terrible shock."

"Marie's tough and very capable," Helene says. "That's why she and Michelle could work together so well. I just do what I'm told, don't I Marie?" Both women exchange smiles. "Don't worry, Danielle, we'll be okay. Somewhere amongst this mess is a bottle of brandy. If everything becomes too much for me, I'll lock the door and drink myself into oblivion."

"Oh no, you won't," Marie says sternly. "Look, I've found the coffee pot," she adds triumphantly. "Now we're saved."

Paul and I leave them to get on with things. There's nothing else to be done. When I arrive back at the office, Laurent informs me that Detective Gerard has called and he wants me to phone him back. Merde, I think, that's all I need.

Things don't improve in the afternoon; quite the reverse in fact. Although Michelle was not liked, people are outraged by her murder, and even worse than that, the attacks on Boutiere's and Michelle's offices. Everyone is talking about it and they all have opinions about what I should do. I hold a high position of respect in this town, but my halo seems to be slipping and I'm in real danger of being criticised. I'm still trying to dodge Detective Gerard's attention, but by late afternoon he tracks me down, once again appearing unexpectedly.

"Bonjour, Sir," I say. "Come into my office. Coffee, Laurent, please." I pull out a chair and Gerard sits. "My, my, two visits in one month, people will talk," I say, trying to lighten the atmosphere. He smiles, but it is more like a grimace. The coffees duly arrive and Laurent leaves, closing the door as he goes. I feel trapped. My sanctuary has been invaded and I've nowhere else to go. My back is literally against the wall.

"I'm under immense pressure, Danielle," he begins. "I don't need to tell you murder is a very serious business, you've dealt with more than your fair share, and very successfully, if I may say. I'm aware that very little time has elapsed and you and your team are carrying out the investigations to the letter, but I'm being squeezed for answers. I don't know what else to say."

"Sir," I reply, "I'm pursuing one definite line of enquiry. A violent loan shark is in some way involved and I sincerely hope I can prove that he's our man, but you must give me time to look at every aspect of the case. There is always a chance that this had nothing to do with money." I feel I must plant this thought in his mind, just in case my killer turns out to be Jacques.

"A crime of passion, perhaps. Maybe her lover is involved? I must admit I was rather startled when I found out about my cousin's living arrangements."

"Yes, it shocked everyone," I lie. "Jacques and Michelle seemed to be such a happy couple."

"So, the two leads you're following are the loan shark and the lover? Good, good," he says. "My family just need to know Jacques is in the clear. We cannot have this awful crime hanging over us and especially not with my position. You do understand, Danielle, don't you?"

What can I say? I'm practically being ordered to find Jacques not guilty of any crime.

"I understand completely, Sir," is all I can reply. "I'm sure before very long, we'll have the answers we need."

He stands, shakes my hand and we walk to the door, but before I open it to show him out he says, "I'm counting on you, Danielle. Don't let me down." There is an edge to his voice. Something about his tone is slightly menacing and when I close the door behind him, I'm left with a bad taste in my mouth and a feeling of unease.

Chapter 19

"But what will I do if he phones me? I know nothing?" Patricia says.

"Tell him you know nothing," I reply.

"What if he pays me a visit and I'm on my own? What will I do?"

"You don't open the door and you call me."

"But what if he smashes it down?"

"Oh, for goodness sake Patricia! Gonzales simply spoke to Claude and he was close to Michelle. Why should he be any different with you?" I'm getting upset, but not with Patricia. I warned her about Juan Gonzales and now she's scared and I'm scared for her. Her eyes fill with tears that threaten, at any moment, to spill down her cheeks. Ollee, seeing her distress, runs over to comfort her. He places his paws on her lap, gives a concerned 'yip' then tries to lick her cheeks. I pace the floor of our kitchen. I'm annoyed with myself for upsetting her, but I don't know what to say. Any words of comfort that I do impart might have me blubbering. She cuddles the dog and kisses his head.

"What if he has a gun? What if he shoots Ollee to get to me? I couldn't bear it if he hurt Ollee."

"No one is going to hurt Ollee and no one is going to hurt you. I'm going to track down this man today and that will be the end of it. I'm ninety-nine per cent sure he had nothing to do with Michelle's death. I think her murder was a crime of passion."

"It's the other one per cent that's worries me," she replies.

"Anyway, what are your plans for today?" I ask, trying to change the subject.

"I'm having lunch with Claude, but first we're going to the studio that Michelle rented. We've got a tenant moving in tomorrow and we just want to do a last-minute check to make sure everything's in order."

Where and when will you be having lunch? I'll join you, if you'd like."

"Cedric's," she replies. "I'd love it if you can manage the time to meet us. I'll even treat you to lunch."

"You're offering to pay? Wow, it's really great having such a wealthy friend," I reply. "Lunch at Cedric's, that's almost as good as the Eiffel Tower restaurant."

"For being so cheeky, I withdraw my generous offer. You can pay for lunch and some wine. Make that the best wine," she adds. The mood is lifted, there is no more talk of Juan Gonzales and I'm relieved.

We chat for a few minutes more then I leave the comfortable coolness of the house and climb into the claustrophobic stuffiness of my car. It's on stifling days like today when I wish I had an open-topped vehicle. I drive with all the windows and the roof light open, but it does little to help as the air is so hot. I feel as if I'm driving with a hairdryer blasting heat at my face. When I arrive at my office, it's not much better. Practically the entire front of the building is made of glass and the heat builds up very quickly. Paul and Laurent have the door wedged open and each have an electric fan on their desk, pointed at their faces. They are sweating profusely.

"When we were at school, the teacher held our lessons outside on days like this," Paul says. "Is there any outside work I can volunteer for?"

"I'd like to be considered for outside work too," Laurent says. "Anything to get out of this stifling hole. Now I know how Michelle Moliner must have felt. This office is like a sauna."

I hadn't considered what Michelle must have gone through in her final minutes, but now I shudder. What a terrible death it must have been.

"I have to be out at lunchtime," I say to the boys. "Both of you disappear for an hour and I'll look after the shop. Just one hour, mind you, then I need you back here. Don't go far, I'll phone you if anything turns up that we have to attend."

Everything is unusually quite while they are out, but within a couple of minutes of their return both the office phone and my mobile begin to ring. Paul picks up the phone and signals that it's an emergency call. When I look at the screen on my mobile I see my call is from Patricia and cold chills run down my spine. I instinctively suspect something is wrong.

"Danielle, it's me, I need you. Please come and help me. I'm at the studio with Claude."

Paul hands me a hastily scribbled note. The address is for the apartment block owned by Patricia and Monsieur Claude. Underneath the word 'body' is written.

"Don't worry, darling, I'm on my way. Don't touch anything," I reply.

My hands are shaking as I collect my bag. I leave Laurent in the office and Paul and I make our way around the corner to the apartment block. He is grimly silent as we walk. I too say nothing, but my heart is pounding so hard the noise of it fills my ears. When we enter the building Patricia and Claude are standing in the hall outside the door of the studio. They are both white faced.

"He's on the floor beside the bed," Claude says. "There's blood running out of his ear."

"It's Michelle's lover," Patricia says. "I don't know how he got into the apartment. We took away his keys when we asked him to leave."

"There's an empty briefcase beside him on the floor. The lock's been prised open," Claude adds.

"Have you touched anything?" I ask them.

"No, nothing," Claude responds.

"I just checked the body," Patricia says. "The room is clean and tidy, nothing is out of place."

"And you're sure he's dead?"

A small hiccupping sob escapes Patricia's throat and I realise she's barely holding it together.

"I think after years of working for a funeral house, I'm more than qualified to know when someone is dead," she says. "Besides, the body is already cold."

The front door of the building is opened and we can hear voices in the hallway. Paul goes to investigate and returns a couple of minutes later.

"Tourists," he says, "Just returning to their apartment. I said there's been an accident and everything is okay."

"This is all we need at the height of the tourist season," Claude says miserably. "I know this is a crime scene, Danielle, but can you keep things as low key as possible? Perhaps avoid taping off the hallway with police line tape? I don't want our guests to be in fear for their lives. It could be very bad for business."

Both Claude and Patricia look sick and their faces are gaunt.

"Why don't you two go across the road to the café and get some coffee, and I'll join you when I can," I suggest. "There's nothing to be done here now."

They both nod their agreement. "If you're sure that's okay," Monsieur Claude says. "I could certainly use a drink."

He gently takes Patricia's elbow and guides her towards the exit. She turns to me before leaving the building, "Thank you," she mouths.

Paul and I enter the room and look at the body. We both confirm it is Guy Legler.

"I don't know if this new development helps or hinders our inquiry," Paul says. "Are we looking for one murderer or two, I wonder?"

"Michelle was cooked and this one's had his head staved in," I say. "Two different methods of killing. Also, there was nothing taken at Michelle's house whereas someone prised open that briefcase," I add.

"You still think the first killing was a crime of passion," he states. "And this?"

"This one is about money," I reply. "Michelle used to collect money from Juan Gonzales in a briefcase. I think whoever did this thought that case was full of money, and maybe it was. We'll never know. We'll also never know if Legler found the case here or brought it with him. The only thing we know for sure is that he's dead and we now have two murders to solve."

"Either the killer found what he was after, or something must have disturbed him – otherwise this room would have been turned over," Paul notes. "As Patricia said, nothing is out of place."

I glance in the wardrobe. The fitted safe is still there and it's still locked. Perhaps Guy had custody of the 200,000 euros from the last transaction which might never have been completed, but what about the 50,000 euros that Michelle stole from Gonzales. Could that money be hidden in the safe, I wonder?

Chapter 20

We have only to wait fifteen minutes before the arrival of Doctor Poullet. A metallic scraping noise as he parks his car facing the wrong way, alongside an iron railing, heralds his arrival. I can't bear to look.

Paul laughs. "There soon won't be a single bit of his car without a scrape or a dent," he remarks. "How long can he continue driving like that before he loses his licence or worse, injures someone?"

"Well he hasn't hurt anyone yet," I state, defending my friend. "There are worse drivers than Poullet on the road. At least he's sober."

Poullet gets out of his car, muttering under his breath as he waddles towards us.

"Well, what are you waiting for? I don't have all day. Show the dog the rabbit," he says.

We lead him into the studio and I point to the body on the floor. "There is blood coming out of his ear. I think he's been bashed on the head," I say.

"Congratulations, Danielle! Forgive me for not saying something sooner, but I didn't realise you'd qualified as a doctor since we last met," he replies sarcastically.

Paul chuckles before Poullet turns on him. "I suppose you too, have hidden talents. Perhaps you double as a psychiatrist or maybe a dentist?" He studies the position of the body. "Humph, at least this one had the courtesy to lie down on the floor and expire, in a clean and tidy apartment. For once, I don't have to walk through mud or climb half way up a mountain."

Paul looks as if he's going to say something, but I throw him a stern stare to warn him. He thinks better of it and clamps his jaws shut.

"You are wrong," Poullet states. "This man was not bashed on the head. I've examined his skull and there is no visible sign of impact. I think he was punched hard on the temple at the left-hand side. There is a mark from a ring. I think a single punch ended this man's life. Whoever hit him must have been a 'Goliath'. I'll know better once I open him up and remove his brain. A bludgeon to the head indeed; everyone has an opinion, everyone is an expert."

He continues to mutter and grumble. Paul and I wait in silence. Eventually, he is finished. Poullet removes his latex gloves, sighs audibly then makes for the door. "You can have the body removed," he says. "I'll give you my report when I'm good and ready."

"Grumpy old bastard," Paul says, once Poullet exits the apartment.

Suddenly his head appears back around the door. "I can assure you, my parents were married," he announces to a startled Paul. "And you too would be grumpy if you had to work with an idiot, Officer," he adds, looking pointedly at Paul who blushes deeply. "I'll thank you to remember my position in future and your manners."

Paul's mouth is open, he looks sick. Poullet winks at me and smiles. Bad old devil, I think and I remember why I like him so much.

I send Paul across the road to the café, to get a key from Claude so we can secure the apartment. When he returns, I say, "After you're finished here, lock up and bring me the key. I'll be at the café or I'll be at my home. Tell Laurent he's to close the office tonight."

I want the key so I can return here when I'm on my own. One way or another, I plan to open the safe and I don't want anyone to know if I discover money hidden there.

When I cross the road to the café I see Claude and Patricia seated at a table near the door. As soon as I join them, Cedric brings me a coffee.

"Terrible business," he says. "Patricia told me all about it, but I've said nothing." He pats the side of his nose with his extended forefinger.

"Don't worry Cedric," I say. "The word will soon be out. We think he may have fallen and struck his head."

"Ah, an accident then," Cedric replies, and he sounds disappointed.

Patricia stares at me, frowning, and I meet her eyes slowly shaking my head to indicate that I'm lying. Claude sees the look pass between us and he knows to keep quiet. Why panic people unnecessarily.

When Cedric moves away I ask, "Do either of you know the combination of the safe that's in the wardrobe?"

"There is a master code," Patricia replies. "I have it in a file at home. They gave it to me when I purchased the safes, back when we were carrying out the renovations. It overrides any code that's been set. Just in case someone places their valuables inside then forgets the combination."

"It makes sense for us to be able to open them," Claude adds. "We get so many elderly people visiting the spa and some of them have dementia. Then of course, there are others who are simply rather stupid."

"I need to ensure Michelle left nothing in it, no incriminating evidence," I say.

"You think there might be paperwork that will point to her killer?" Claude asks.

"No," I reply. "I think it will be empty, but I have to check just in case."

I get a rush of excitement at the prospect of finding something valuable. There's not a minute to lose, however, as I'm sure it'll be only a matter of time before Gonzales returns with a crowbar so he can remove the safe and finish the job he started.

Chapter 21

I don't want to rush Patricia when she's been so upset, but I'm anxious for her to finish her coffee so I can drive her home to look for the safe code. All the while we are sitting at Cedric's, people are coming over to ask what has happened. Patricia and Claude are sticking to my story of an accident taking place, but I know it won't be long until the truth comes out. I've paid for the coffees and we are standing ready to leave when an ambulance arrives to remove the body and a whole new wave of enquiries begins.

"I'm sorry, Patricia, Claude," I say. "But we'll have to leave now. I need the code for the safe and if you're ready Patricia, I can drive you home and collect it at the same time."

Tuesday is normally my day off, but I've been so busy since Michelle's death I've not stopped, so I'm feeling rather tired and irritable. By the time everyone has said goodbye, the ambulance drivers emerge from the building with the body then Paul runs across with the keys.

"Good timing, Boss," he says. "Another couple of minutes and I'd have missed you. I've telephoned Laurent to tell him he's locking up tonight. What do you want me to do now? Do you want me to accompany you somewhere? Or is there anyone you want me to talk to?"

I turn to Claude. "Could you go to the office with Paul just now? Do you have the time to give him your statement? We can see you tomorrow otherwise."

"I've a really busy day tomorrow, Danielle," he replies. "I don't plan on going back to work today because I'm still rather upset, so I'll go to your office now. Not that I can tell you much, there's not much to tell."

"Take Monsieur Claude to the office and type up his statement for signing. There's a bottle of brandy in my desk drawer. Make sure you pour him a generous measure because he's had a bad shock," I say.

"Thank you, Danielle," Claude replies. "You're right, it has been a terrible shock."

That should keep them busy for a while, I think. Claude enjoys his brandy and he'll want to share his ordeal with Laurent and anyone else who comes into the office who'll listen. If I'm quick, I can drive Patricia home, pick up the code and be back here in under half an hour. Then I can open the safe without the risk of Claude, or anyone else, disturbing me. I assume if Gonzales returns, it's more likely to happen at night and I'd rather avoid that encounter.

When we arrive back home, Ollee greets us with his usual enthusiasm. Mimi the cat lifts her head from her comfy position. She is lying along the back of my armchair. Mimi stretches her legs until her tail trembles then she relaxes once again and goes back to sleep. What an easy life our cat has, I think. Patricia switches on the coffee pot then begins to slice one of her delicious apple pies. I am too edgy to eat or drink anything, and although I don't want to upset Patricia, I find myself nagging her to find me the code.

"The sooner I leave the sooner I'll be back," I say. "Then we can both relax. When I return, I'll set the table in the garden and we can dine in the fresh air and I'll buy a bottle of that good red wine from the *cave*. Today should really be my day off and I'm beginning to run out of steam."

My final comment does the trick. "I'm sorry, Danielle," Patricia says. "Of course you must be tired. I'll fetch that number right now and don't worry, by the time you return I'll have the table set and the food prepared. When you go to buy the wine, pick up two bottles," she adds.

After rooting around in the filing cabinet then flicking through volumes of paper, she eventually finds what she's looking for. "Voila," she says triumphantly. "I have it."

I feel as if we've been home for ages, but only ten minutes have elapsed. I take the paper, practically snatching it out of her hand and head back out the door. "Back soon," I call, almost as an afterthought.

I try not to drive like a maniac, but I'm anxious to return to the studio. I keep getting a rush of excitement every time I think about opening the safe. The road is busy, mostly with British tourists, if the number of right-hand drive cars is anything to go by. They haven't yet mastered our narrow mountain roads and seem to travel down the middle instead of keeping to their own side. By the time I reach town, my hands are sweating from gripping the steering wheel and my head is sore. I park illegally on yellow lines, but have the comfort of knowing my car won't be ticketed. With the apartment keys in my hand and the code in my bag, I enter the building and make for the studio.

My hands are shaking when I open the door, but I'm careful to close it behind me then lock it, leaving the key in place. My heart is pounding as I punch in the code number for the safe. For a split-second nothing happens then I hear an electronic whirring sound like barrels spinning round, then there is a 'ping' and the door pops open. I feel a surge of excitement as I reach out and pull the door fully open. I'm expecting to see piles of money, but I'm dreadfully disappointed. Instead, there is a small brown envelope. On inspection, it contains nothing more than a locker key. I could cry. I lie back on the floor until my heart rate returns to normal and I can think coherently once again. I have no idea where the key fits; it could be for a locker anywhere.

My heart is not in it when I go to buy the wine, but I dutifully pick up the two bottles Patricia has requested. In reality, I'm no worse off than I was before, except before I had expectation and hope. When I arrive back home I place the wine and the locker key on the kitchen table and admire the wonderful spread of food Patricia is assembling for our meal.

"Why were you at the spa?" Patricia asks. "I thought you were just going to the studio."

"What do you mean?" I reply. "I didn't go to the spa. What made you think I was there?"

"The locker key, the purple key fob is from the spa. I ordered them for Claude last month because the ones he was using were so worn out, you couldn't make out the numbers."

With expectation and hope restored I take Patricia's sweet face in my hands and kiss both her cheeks. When I look at my watch I see that the spa will still be open. I grab the key from the table and leaving a mystified Patricia in my wake, run back to my car.

If Claude has returned to his office he won't see me when I enter the locker room and even if he does notice me, I'll simply say I was coming to check on him. Adrenalin is rushing through my veins once more. It's very hot and by the time I enter the spa my clothes are stuck to my body uncomfortably. Coming out of the brightness of the sun, the hallway seems very dark.

"Bonjour, Danielle," Madame Georges, the secretary says. Her voice startles me and I jump. "If you are here to see Monsieur Claude, he's not returning tonight. He telephoned to tell me about the accident at the apartment. Can I help you with anything?"

"No, thank you, I just came to check on Monsieur Claude," I say. I hadn't anticipated Madame Georges being in the corridor outside the offices.

At that moment, a client comes up to us to ask Madame Georges something about his appointments. I am saved.

"If you'll excuse me, Danielle," she says. "I'll leave you to see yourself out while I take Monsieur Reynard to my office. I'll tell Monsieur Claude you called."

As soon as she is out of sight, I rush into the locker room. It's empty, probably because it's near the end of the day. Quickly, I locate the correct locker and open it with the key. There is a canvas bag inside. I'm shaking like a leaf as I grab the bag then exit the room, leaving the key in the open locker for the next person to use.

I return to my car, place the bag on the passenger seat then drive a short distance outside town where I can't be watched, before reaching for the bag and unzipping it. It is full of used bank notes, piles and piles of money. Tears fill my eyes. I stare and stare, then gently caress the notes. Nobody knows about this money. If I keep it no one will ever know. There's a fortune in the bag. All I have to do is find a way of cleaning it up. Perhaps I'll investigate buying property over the border in Spain just like Juan Gonzales, or use this cash for smaller transactions like clothes or shopping or paying household bills. There's enough money to last me for years and years to come.

I take a hundred euros out of the bag and stuff the notes into my wallet. Then I zip up the bag and lock it in the boot. I manage to calm myself down, restart the engine, turn my car around and head back to town. I'll surprise Patricia and buy a good bottle of champagne, I think, she deserves it, and I can't help grinning like an idiot as I drive.

Chapter 22

"And you're sure we can keep the money?" Patricia asks. "Are you absolutely certain no one will know we have it and no one will have a claim on it?"

"The only person who knows anything about it is Juan Gonzales, the loan shark. He extricated the cash from vulnerable people so he doesn't deserve to have it. Michelle Moliner is dead. She stole fifty thousand euros from Gonzales, but apart from Pascal Boutiere, who's keeping his mouth shut, nobody knows anything about that. Once we go inside and count the money, we'll see how much we have, but from the weight of it I'm sure it's more than fifty thousand euros."

"I don't want to take any chances, Danielle. We're already comfortably well off. Nothing is worth putting our lives in danger. What if Gonzales gets in touch and asks me about the safe? If he's the person who killed Guy Legler, then he must have noticed the safe closed and locked. What if he breaks in and sees it's now open and empty?"

"Trust me, Patricia I'll catch up with Gonzales. We won't be in any danger. He's clutching at straws. Besides, Claude's already told him you know nothing."

"And what about the studio, can we rent it to a tourist? Wouldn't they be at risk? Gonzales might come back there."

"Right now, it's a crime scene, but when forensics release it, leave it empty, put your tourist into another apartment, any other apartment, even if it means giving business to someone else. I'll pay the rent on the studio if necessary until the case is solved or closed. You can bill me for it. As long as Claude sees the money coming in, he'll be happy. I think I can just about afford to pay," I say and we smile at each other nervously.

We're both rather apprehensive about opening the bag and properly checking its contents. We know it's full of money, but it seems a bit unreal. I play with the food on my plate pushing it around with the fork. My stomach is cramping with nerves.

"Finish your food, Danielle, I can't wait to go inside and count our money," Patricia says excitedly. I've managed to reassure her and the prospect of all that money has strengthened my resolve.

"I can't wait either," I reply. "Let's just clear this table and we can finish eating in the kitchen."

When we're seated at the kitchen table I tip out the contents of the bag. Bundles of notes fall in a heap and several loose bills slide onto the floor, causing Ollee to bark. Patricia and I can't stop grinning at our haul.

"This calls for champagne," I say happily. I fetch two glasses and open the bottle. Then we begin to count.

When the counting is complete we have finished the champagne and one of the bottles of red wine, we are rather intoxicated and two hundred and forty-six thousand euros better off.

"We have to hide this money, Danielle," Patricia says nervously. "What if someone breaks in? We can't put it in a bank. What will we do with it?"

"Firstly, we'll put it back in the bag," I say. "We want it out of sight in case someone drops in to visit us. Then tonight, when I go to bed, I'll tuck the money under the duvet beside me. By tomorrow, when I'm less intoxicated, I'll have a plan."

Patricia begins to laugh. "You're going to sleep with the money," she says. "Well I think I'll join you. It's not every day you get to share your bed with a fortune."

We both start to laugh at the prospect and Ollee starts making yipping barks then he takes off, running around and around in circles. Patricia speaks kindly to the excitable dog, trying to calm him down. I'm sure he too, will end up sharing my bed.

Surprisingly, I wake bright and early on Wednesday morning and I've thought of a perfect place to hide the cash. When our chicken house was originally built, it had been constructed as an apple store. Under the stone floor is a 'cave'. It's not very big and I think it probably held bottles and jars. If I place the bag of money in an airtight, plastic container and hide it in the 'cave', nobody would ever suspect it was there. There is a paving stone which can be lifted to give access, but only I know of its existence. It's a perfect solution.

Before I leave for work I take five thousand euros from the bag then stash the rest of the money in the 'cave'. Patricia and I agree that this money will be used as and when we require it to pay for anything we need. We can pay our legitimate, earned money into the bank. I place five hundred euros in my wallet, give the balance to Patricia to store in the house and leave for work. I've never carried this much cash around to cover my day to day expenses before, but I like the warm feeling the money gives me and I know I'll soon get used to it.

After I leave my colleagues some work to be getting on with, I walk around to the studio to see if anything has been disturbed. It dawns on me that we didn't find any keys to the apartment when we found Legler dead inside, and as the door wasn't broken, I can only assume he'd had a copy made which the killer removed. I make a mental note to advise Claude to change the locks. When I enter the studio, all is exactly as I'd left it. Not wishing to rush back to the stifling confines of the office I walk towards the café to see if my friend Byron is in his usual place, seated beside the door. If he is there, I plan to buy us both some coffee. My new-found wealth is burning a hole in my pocket.

As I near the dog grooming parlour, I see Sarah standing in the street outside. She's struggling to assemble a small advertising board while at the same time holding onto the leads of four dogs. I reach out when I am alongside her and help her to erect the board.

"Oh, thank you Danielle, I was finding everything a bit difficult," she says. "As you know, it's the annual dog show this Saturday and the owner of the grooming parlour has very kindly offered to help me promote the animal shelter. This sign is to let everyone know how to contact me, in case someone wishes to re-home one of these beautiful boys. See, their photos are pinned to the board."

I look at the four mutts she has charge of and the word 'beautiful' is the farthest thing from my lips. One is very tall and skinny and is sadly missing most of his tail. Another has short, bandy legs, a fat body and an enormous head. The third is barking at every passer-by. He is elderly and grumpy and snarling, showing what's left of his teeth. The fourth is a grey-coloured lump of matted fur.

Sarah catches sight of my expression and says, "Benny lost his tail in an accident, Carlos is being put on a diet, Pepe isn't bad-tempered he's just scared and poor Freddy is here for a hair cut. He's quite a small dog, but his previous owner never brushed him or had him trimmed. The shelter is very short of cash. If I can't find homes for these boys or raise money from donations, I don't know how I'll feed them. Some people are so cruel to their animals and nobody seems to care if a dog goes hungry. Life is so unfair. Your Ollee is a very lucky boy to live with you and Patricia. He's very lucky indeed."

If Sarah was trying to tug at my heart strings with the mention of Ollee, she's succeeded. I reach into my bag, remove my wallet and take one hundred euros from it.

"This will feed your dogs for a while," I say, handing her the money. "It's a donation from me and Patricia to start off the fundraising. Good luck with the shelter."

Sarah's eyes immediately fill with tears. "This is a hundred euros, Danielle! Did you mean to give me this much money?"

"Take it with our blessing," I reply. "Someone has to recognise the sacrifices you're making for these dumb animals."

I enjoy the extravagance of handing over such a large sum of cash. It gives me a buzz.

She hugs me and kisses both my cheeks. Fat, bandy dog is peeing on tall, skinny dog's feet. Small angry dog is trying to bite my shoulder bag.

"Behave, Pepe," Sarah says, tugging on his collar.

Her legs are tied up with the tangled leads as the creatures walk about in different directions, but I've had enough of ugly dogs so I leave her to sort it out. When I reach the café, Byron is there and I join him. He's pleased to see me.

"Hello, dear girl," he says. "And to what do I owe this pleasure?"

"Oh, you know, Byron. The sun is shining and my colleagues are handling the work, so I thought I'd spend some time drinking coffee with my friend."

We sit and chat for a while then Marie comes along and we greet her. She sits down at our table.

"How are things going at the agency?" I ask.

"Difficult," she replies. "I had to take a break. It was much easier to work for Michelle than Helene. I understood her better, even though she was tougher."

"And how is Helene coping without her sister?" Byron asks.

"Quite well, actually," Marie says. "She's running her sister's business. She's installed herself in her sister's grand house and she's living with her sister's husband. Did you know she's given up her flat and moved in with Jacques permanently?"

Byron and I exchange glances. "Didn't I hear that Jacques once courted Helene, before Michelle came on the scene?" I say.

"They were practically engaged," Marie replies. "But he couldn't resist Michelle's charms. She was the prettier one when they were younger and she dazzled him with her flashing eyes and her quick wit. Helene didn't stand a chance. Their parents didn't care which one of their daughters he married, just so long as he married one of them. He had money, you see. Now Helene has everything which should rightfully have been hers from the start," she adds. "Anyway, I'd better get back. The work won't take care of itself and Helene doesn't cope well when I'm not there."

"She seems rather bitter," Byron says. "I bet Marie expected to be put in charge of the agency."

"I'm sure that's the case," I agree.

It sounds to me as if Helene has benefited rather well from Michelle's death, and I wonder if she knows more about who might have killed her than she's letting on. Maybe it's time to speak to Jacques once again.

Chapter 23

I'm about to order more coffee when my mobile rings. When I answer it, Paul says, "You'd better come back to the office, Boss. There's a woman here who says she's Guy Legler's wife. She wants to claim his personal effects and there's more – she says her name is Antonia Gonzales."

I'm stunned. I hadn't heard anything about Legler having a wife. In fact, we're still trying to trace any family for him.

"Keep her there," I reply. "I'm on my way, I'll be back in a couple of minutes."

I say goodbye to Byron and practically run all the way back to the office. Sitting at Paul's desk and shamelessly flirting with him, is one of the most beautiful women I've ever seen. She is tall, rail thin with elegant hands covered in stunning gold and gemstone rings. Her hair is long and blonde, her skin tanned and her eyes are large and blue. Her full red lips are sexy and when she smiles, Laurent visibly pants with desire. Guy Legler was a good-looking man, but not in her league.

"Bonjour, Madame Gonzales," I say. "Please come into my office." I point to my open door.

She slowly uncrosses her legs, rises lazily and walks towards my room. As she walks all eyes are on her swaying hips, even mine – it's mesmerising. When we are seated and the door is shut I say, "I'm sorry for your loss, Madame. We had no idea Monsieur Legler was married or we would have contacted you right away. "How did you find out about his death?"

She doesn't bat an eyelid; nothing seems to faze her. "My brother was in town and he heard about Guy and telephoned me. We live in Cadaqués and I was surprised when Guy didn't return home, but we had an open marriage so I didn't really worry. Guy often spent time away."

"Presumably, you knew about his affairs," I say.

"Oh, yes, as I said, we had an open marriage. Our little affairs kept our love life fresh."

Has this woman no shame, I wonder?

"I'd like to collect Guy's personal belongings now if you don't mind," she says. "I believe he had an overnight bag. Did you find it? It contains some papers belonging to my brother."

"Firstly, I cannot release anything of Monsieur Legler's without proper documentation being produced. I'll need your identity papers, you wedding certificate, proof of address etc. Secondly, because we believe your husband was murdered, nothing can happen until the inquiry is complete."

"Murdered?" she repeats. "Juan told me he'd had an accident and banged his head. That's the story I heard in town, as well."

Her forehead is furrowed with frown lines and her mouth is slack, but she quickly regains her composure.

"So, Juan Gonzales is your brother," I state. "I'd like to speak to him. Do you know where he is?"

Her eyes widen. "He's not here, he's gone back to Spain," she replies. "Why do you want to speak to him? He had nothing to do with this. He and Guy worked together. They were friends, close friends."

"Madame, your brother smashed up the office of the *notaire*. He's been trying to locate a large sum of money that he says is missing. I think that money was being held on his behalf by a local estate agent called Madame Moliner. She too, has been murdered. Your husband was killed by a single punch to the head. It takes great strength to deliver such a blow and your brother is a big and powerful man. Two people who Juan had dealings with are now dead and he's had a violent encounter with a third. Who do you think is the most likely candidate for these crimes?"

Her face hardens. "So, you're not going to give me my husband's belongings. How can I get a list of what you're holding and how do I apply to have them returned to me?"

"We'll write to you in due course if you leave your details with my colleague. Although I can tell you now that we found nothing other than the clothes he was wearing and a wallet containing a few euros in his pocket. There was no overnight bag and his keys were missing."

"Did you search the room? The cupboards and the drawers? Guy told me there was a safe in the wardrobe, did you search it?"

"The room was completely empty and so was the safe. As I said, he had nothing with him."

She is clearly agitated and annoyed. She stands to leave.

"If you speak to your brother, please tell him I want to talk to him," I say. "Ask him to report here. The *notaire* might want to press charges for the damages he caused."

Her eyes are black with rage and her face is stiff and ugly. "Will that be all?" she asks through gritted teeth. "May I leave now?"

"Of course, Madame," I reply. "You came here to speak to me. I didn't summon you. Of course, you are free to leave."

Without saying another word, she storms out of my room, through the outer office and out of the front door. I guess she's changed her mind about leaving us her contact details.

I ask Paul to circulate Juan Gonzales's details throughout the region and over the border with our colleagues in Spain. I believe I have enough evidence to charge him with assault and malicious damage and I also intimate that we wish to question him about two murders. Then I email a report to Detective Gerard, advising him of the same. Almost instantaneously he replies by telephoning me.

"Well done, Danielle," he says. "I'm so relieved we have our man. Good police work, very good work."

He's so delighted, I don't want to burst his bubble by repeating that I think Michelle's murder is a crime of passion and nothing to do with Gonzales. I let him chatter on, promising me this and that. In his eyes, I've solved all the crimes, now all I have to do is bring them to fruition.

Chapter 24

The end of the week is rather quiet after the excitement at the start. Poullet's report confirms that Legler's death was caused by a blow to the temple, which resulted in a brain haemorrhage. There has been no sign of Juan Gonzales or his sister. Stupid tourists have continued to do stupid things. Sarah has told everyone about my generous donation to the animal shelter. I'll have to be more careful, I think. I don't want people to know I've suddenly come into a lot of money.

Patricia is preparing for the dog show which is tomorrow. She thinks Ollee can win the section for the cleverest dog and has been teaching him tricks. I've decided to give myself the day off tomorrow so I may attend the show with her, now that my work has become less frantic. Monday will be soon enough to attempt to contact Antonia Gonzales about her husband's body. In fact, I think I'll take Patricia and Ollee to Cadaqués to look for her. We'll have a lovely lunch at a beachside restaurant and I'll charge it to expenses. If I can't contact Madame Gonzales, and I don't intend to try too hard, I'll pass the task on to my head office in Perpignan.

Eventually, someone somewhere will discover the whereabouts of Juan Gonzales and with a bit of luck, it won't be me. I've already received accolades for discovering the identity of the killer. I don't have to be around for his arrest. Now I have the money and Juan thinks it is still lost somewhere in the ether, I don't really care what happens to the rest of the people involved.

My mobile rings and I see the caller is Patricia. "Bonjour, Danielle," she says. "I need a favour please, if you can spare the time. I've tried to phone but the line is constantly engaged and soon it will be too late."

"Yes, darling, what can I do to help you?" I ask.

"It's Ollee, he needs a bath and a trim, but I can't get through to the grooming parlour on the phone because it's constantly busy and I don't want to bring him into town unless I'm sure they can fit him in."

Ollee is one of the oddest dogs I've ever seen. He wouldn't win any beauty contests, even if a top stylist trimmed his wild coat. He has tufts going in all directions and a ridiculous tail. He looks as if he's been made from the rejected bits of other dogs, but Patricia adores him so what can I do?

"I'll run around right now, darling and I'll phone you straight back. If they can fit him in, I'll drive up and collect you. I've plenty of time today. Oh, and by the way, tomorrow is going to be my day off so I'll come with you to see our dog triumph in the show."

I'm smiling as I say this. I think I'll see a flying pig before our crazy mutt wins anything in a dog show, but Patricia can't see my sarcastic expression so she's delighted by my support.

When I arrive at the grooming parlour there's a queue outside. Bitches are barking and snapping and growling and whining and that's just the owners. Oh, mon Dieu, I'm not sure what to do. I don't want to let Patricia down.

"Police business, let me pass," I say, fighting my way through the tangle of women, dogs, leads and handbags. "Make room please – out of my way, ladies or I'll have to move you on. You're blocking the pavement."

Reluctantly, the queue parts and I squeeze through the narrow door and go inside. A small trembling ball of fluff is in a harness, which is suspended from the ceiling. His paws are barely touching the table he's standing on. Two women are working on him. One is using a hair dryer while the other is buffing his nails. When he sees me, he whimpers, but I think he knows I'm not here to save him. Marylene, the owner and wielder of the nail buffer, looks up.

"Danielle, hello, how are you? What can I do for you? Sorry I can't stop, you see how it is, but I can answer if you need to talk to me."

"Marylene, I need a huge favour," I say. "It's Patricia's dog, Ollee. He's not very beautiful, in fact he's rather odd-looking and I don't really see how anyone can improve his appearance, but Patricia believes you can. Is there any way you could give him a bath and trim some of the tufts over his eyes so he looks a bit more normal? Patricia's entering him in the cleverest dog section in tomorrow's show."

She glances at her appointment book. "If she can get him here in twenty minutes I'll fit him in. Madame Dupont has cancelled her girl's appointment because she's pregnant— the dog, not Madame Dupont," she explains. "She's only bringing her boy in for a trim. So yes, the answer is yes, providing she's here in twenty minutes. Any later and there's no chance."

I phone Patricia as I hurry towards the car park.

"Remember to pay with cash," I say. "Put some cash in your handbag. Make sure you're ready to get straight into my car or we won't make it. For the record, I don't think Ollee is going to enjoy this and I like the way he looks now. You can't improve on perfection."

"You're very kind, Danielle," she replies. "And of course, he's perfect, but I'm sure he'll feel better after a bath. He'll certainly smell better."

My sweet girl just doesn't get my sense of humour, I think, and it's probably just as well.

I feel like a traitor when I drop Patricia and Ollee off at the grooming parlour, more so because Ollee is so happy to be in town and socialising with the other dogs. He sniffs the air and the pavement and the other victims who are standing in line and I can't get away quickly enough. Patricia says she'll walk home with Ollee after the deed is done to give him some exercise, so I won't have to face him until I get home.

When I return to the office I receive a call from Pascal Boutiere. He advises me that when he went through Michelle's files, he discovered a bank account in the name of Guy Legler containing six thousand euros.

"She must have given him the money, but he hasn't touched any of it. I suppose it now belongs to his beneficiaries," he says.

If I do find Antonia Gonzales in Cadaqués, she might actually be pleased to see me.

Chapter 25

I'd worried needlessly about Ollee, as Patricia tells me he enjoyed all the attention and pampering. Seeing him powdered and perfumed and with the fur on his head trimmed, I must admit he looks and smells much better than before. Now it's possible to see his beautiful, gentle eyes without spikes of unruly hair masking them.

The dog show is bedlam, but Sarah is in her element. Benny, Carlos and Freddy have all found homes, only Pepe remains unwanted, and no wonder, who in their right mind would willingly take in an old, bad-tempered mongrel as a pet? I hear Patricia talking to Sarah and see that Ollee and Pepe seem to like each other. I'm about to intervene as I'm worried if I don't, Pepe might come home with us, but luckily, for once Patricia listens to her head before her heart.

"I'm sorry, Sarah," she says, "But we simply can't be responsible for any more animals. We already have Ollee, Mimi, chickens and rabbits, and Danielle's Papa is about to re-home six hives of bees to our orchard. Pepe is out of luck today, but at least you've only one dog left, now that the others have found new owners."

Sarah purses her lips and glances at a box which has just been abandoned at her feet containing two scruffy-looking ginger kittens. I don't think she'll ever be free of strays. She's doing the best PR job she can, but try as she might, nobody wants Pepe. I think she's sorry she's taken him on and would love to be rid of the nasty little mutt. Then, probably feeling guilty, she reaches down to pat his head, and true to form, he snaps at her hand. If Pepe doesn't watch his step, he might soon be going on a one-way trip to the vet.

We spend the day watching events, drinking beer and eating grilled pork in baguettes. I'm beginning to tire when we finally reach the point in the show for the cleverest dog competition. There are nine entries in all, with Ollee being second from last to compete. He does as well as he can, given the limited time Patricia has spent training him and we are delighted when he comes second to a Border Collie.

"We've done it, Danielle!" Patricia says delightedly. "Ollee is a champion."

With a rosette tied to his collar and a wide grin on Patricia's face, we make our way home. We've gone less than a hundred metres along the riverbank when Ollee sniffs the air and takes off after a rabbit. The powdered pooch that left us returns covered with earth and pieces of grass. Twigs stick out of his coat and there is a distinct smell of horse manure emanating from him. For a moment, Patricia looks crestfallen, then Ollee wags his tail and starts to leap up at us in an attempt to lick our faces and all we can do is laugh.

"Champion indeed," I say. "I'm afraid this dog will always be an unruly scamp, but to us he's irreplaceable."

While we were at the dog show my Papa, together with his friend Monsieur Purcell and several members of the beekeeping association, have moved the hives to the orchard. On Sunday morning Patricia and I meet him there so he can show off his bees. I'm not keen to get too close, but Papa is so happy and animated I'm delighted for him. We spend several hours hanging out in the orchard, looking at all the equipment and accoutrements necessary for the job. Luckily the tool shed, which is situated quite near the entrance to the land, is large enough to hold everything. Papa has lined up the hives south of the shed to afford them a windbreak, but the land generally offers good shelter and sunlight.

Afterwards, we dine in our garden, still talking about bees until it is almost dark then I drive Papa home. On the way, he finally changes the subject.

"Your Mama and I are thinking about getting a small dog," he says. "Very small, like a poodle or a little terrier. What do you think?"

"Would Mama manage a dog?" I ask. "She's not very strong and they can be a lot of work."

"It's actually your Mama who wants one for the company. We wouldn't get a puppy or even a young dog, but something old like us, something that wouldn't need a lot of exercise. I get to see Ollee quite a lot and I'm always talking about him, but Ollee has too much energy for us. A small, old, lap dog would suit us just fine. The reason I'm asking you is that on some occasions I'd want to bring the dog to the orchard. I just need to be sure you and Patricia would have no objections."

"Papa, I am not the boss of you. You and Mama must decide for yourselves. Patricia and I would be delighted with anything that brings pleasure to your lives. I'll even pay for the start up costs like a bed, lead and food and I'll cover all the vet bills during the dog's lifetime. Call it an early birthday gift for Mama."

Papa is beaming. When I park near his house he says, "Your Mama will be delighted. Will you come in and tell her about your generous gift? She hasn't seen you for a while."

I feel trapped. I can hardly refuse, but I don't get on with my mother very well and I try to avoid confrontations. In the end I do go in, and she is so pleasant to me I can hardly believe it, although all the way home I'm still wondering if I've missed something, some cutting remark or snide comment. In the end, I stop trying to analyse things and just enjoy the moment.

Chapter 26

I rise late on Monday and I'm still not dressed when I telephone the office at opening time to ask Paul to keep an eye on things. After explaining that I'll be driving to Cadaqués to try to trace Antonia Gonzales, and saying that I probably won't be back before close of business, I tell him he can have Wednesday afternoon off so he can attend a car club meeting with Monsieur Claude. It's a peace offering for leaving him in the lurch on the busiest day of the week. I can hear Patricia singing in the kitchen, some repetitive children's song about a dog. Every so often she replaces the word 'dog' with the name 'Ollee' and he barks.

I'm looking forward to driving the coastal road to Cadaqués. If ever there was a day for having an open-topped car, this is it. The narrow, winding roads with spectacular plunging cliff-sides, give uninterrupted views over turquoise bays, and are the stuff movies are made of. A person would feel like James Bond driving along those roads in a sports car and I toy with the idea of buying one with my new-found cash, just for the fun of it.

It's not long before we are on our way and after the excitement of yesterday, Ollee lays down across the back seat and promptly falls asleep. For me the journey is much more peaceful without him trying to balance on Patricia's knees or in the narrow space between the front seats, where from time to time, he attempts to plant his wet tongue in my ear.

"I know you're trying to find Antonia Gonzales in Cadaqués, but do you think there's a risk of encountering her brother?" Patricia asks. "Couldn't that be dangerous? He hasn't tried to get in touch with me about the missing money, although he has spoken to Claude. Shouldn't we just leave well alone and let someone from Perpignan handle this?"

"Every police department in the region is looking for Juan Gonzales. I think he'll be trying to avoid me, more than me avoiding him. He must know by now the money's lost to him. I'm sure we have nothing to worry about," I reply. "Besides, his sister will be delighted when I tell her about her small inheritance."

We continue our journey stopping briefly at Banyuls-sur-Mer and Cerbère so Patricia may take photographs, arriving at Cadaqués in time for lunch. The little town is packed, but eventually I manage to find somewhere to park and we leave the car and head for the beachfront area. Before very long, we are seated in a small restaurant with a view of the sea and dining on a delicious plate of *aile de ray* served with in-season, mixed vegetables. After we dine we walk Ollee down to the beach so he may stretch his legs. Patricia takes my photograph standing alongside the statue of Salvador Dalí, with my hair draped comically in front of my nose like a moustache. Dalí is immortalised by this statue. The people of Cadaqués are very proud of their most famous son, even if the man was mad.

I have a street map of the town and I'm sitting on a bench studying it when I notice Antonia Gonzales seated almost opposite me in a beachfront café. She is hard to miss; her perfect body is relaxing in a chair as she talks on her mobile and sips espresso from a tiny cup. I can't believe my luck at finding her so effortlessly.

"That's the person I'm looking for," I say to Patricia. "The blonde woman, over there."

"Wow, she's gorgeous. Do you think she's gay?"

"Sorry, but I don't think so, she was flirting with Paul in the office. Anyway, she's not so beautiful when she gets angry. Her face becomes really hard and ugly."

"Who cares about her face?" Patricia quips. "Look at that body."

"Down girl," I say. "I'm sorry, but you and Ollee have to stay here. I need to speak to her in private."

Before I get the chance to say any more, Antonia pays her bill and leaves the café.

"I've got to go," I say to Patricia. "I'll telephone your mobile when I'm finished, make sure it's switched on." Then I quickly follow Antonia as she makes her way down a winding street.

We don't walk very far before she enters a little house in the middle of a cul-de-sac. There is hard standing for parking a car to the front of the house, but it's empty, so I assume if Juan stays here he's out at the moment. I'm quaking with nerves as I knock on the door.

"What do you want?" Antonia says rudely when she opens the door and sees me standing outside. "Has something happened with Juan? Is he okay?"

"This isn't about Juan. It's to do with your late husband. There's money involved. He's left you some money. May I come in, or don't you mind your neighbours knowing your business?"

She glances up and down the street then reluctantly lets me enter the house and shows me through a dark hallway and into a large sitting room at the back. The room is light and comfortable, but I'd imagined it would be more opulent than this. It has been furnished by Ikea, with few personal items on show. I see a couple of automatic syringes lying on the coffee table.

"What are those," I ask, pointing to the offending objects. "Have you got a prescription for those drugs?"

"Relax, officer," she replies. "They belong to Juan they're EpiPens, for severe allergic reactions. Juan's allergic to bee stings. He always carries an injector, in case he stung. He's also allergic to dog hair, cat hair, house dust mites and probably a long list of other things, but bees are the worst. They can cause him to go into anaphylactic shock. It seems ridiculous that such a big man can be floored by a tiny creature, but there you are. Now about this money Guy has left?"

I tell her about the bank account and she gives me the information I need to complete my report.

"You do realise," I say, "that we think your brother killed your husband. Don't you find that concerning?"

"If he did, and I don't really believe it to be the case, it must have been an accident. Juan and Guy were best friends. I met Guy through Juan. Juan would never knowingly hurt him."

"Even if money was involved?"

She bites her lower lip. "My husband would never steal money from my brother – never," she stresses. "I think it's time you left. You've given me the news. I'd like you to leave now."

She makes it clear I have no choice. When I'm outside the door I ask, "Does Juan live here too? Is this also his address?"

She doesn't answer, but slams the door in my face rudely.

"I'll find out, you know," I shout with my face pressed against the glass. "I'll find him and I'll arrest him."

I'm met with silence.

"Bitch," I say, banging my fist against the door angrily. Who does she think she is?

Chapter 27

I'm still not satisfied that Juan Gonzales had anything to do with Michelle's murder and I feel I must question Jacques once again, but how to do this without upsetting my boss is a real problem. I decide to make the excuse of wanting to look over any personal papers Michelle kept at the house, to try to establish any contacts she might have had that we've missed.

When I telephone, Helene answers, *"Oui, bonjour,"* she says.

"Bonjour, Madame Lacroix. It's Danielle from the police. Is Jacques there?" I call her Madame even though she has never married, as a mark of respect for her age and position.

"He will be home in half an hour. He's just gone out to post a letter, then he's coming straight back."

I explain why I'm calling.

"There is a desk in the room that was Michelle's study. I have the key now. If you care to call I'll open the drawers for you, but I don't think you'll find anything of significance because Michelle kept most of her contact details in her head. I worked with her and I know very little about her business. Mind you, she often excluded me from her plans."

There is an edge of bitterness in her voice and yet something rather triumphant about what she has said. She has the key now – and everything else, I think. I thank her and arrange to call in an hour's time. I decide to take Paul with me, so can keep Helene and Jacques busy while I nosey around. I'm probably clutching at straws, but you never know what might be hidden away. I might just get lucky.

It is another hot day so I go to the *boulangerie* to buy the croissants for the morning coffees while the boys sit at their desks with fans pointed at their faces. Even though the air is stuffy, it's much better to be outside. As I round the corner, I'm surprised to see my mother walking along the main street. She has a spring in her step instead of her usual hunched shuffle and within a moment or two I understand why. She is holding a lead attached to Pepe. The ugly, bad-tempered dog is snapping and snarling at people as they pass by, making them jump, and my mother is howling with laughter. I'm walking a short distance behind her and praying I can dive into the bakers before she sees me or anyone complains to me about the dog's behaviour.

"I'm not surprised you're hiding, Danielle. I can see you ducking and diving. That horrible tyke just snapped at my leg. Your mother's been up and down the street twice already. It's the most I've ever seen her walk. She's particularly enjoying frightening children and tourists."

Standing in the doorway of the *boulangerie* is Byron. He steps aside to let me enter.

"I'm so sorry, Byron. I had no idea she was re-homing Pepe, or I would have had strong words with Sarah. My Papa said they wanted a small dog. I'm even paying some of the costs, but this dog? Who in their right mind would want this dog?"

"You've just answered your own question. Your mother has always had strange ideas. That ghastly little dog should suit her very well."

Byron waits with me as I make my purchases, then we both leave the shop together. I assume that my mother will have walked to the other end of the street by now, but as I step out onto the pavement I immediately see I'm wrong. She is only a few paces away and is facing towards me so there's no escape.

"Ah, Danielle, bonjour! And bonjour to you too, Monsieur."

"Bonjour, Mama," I reply dutifully.

Byron nods an acknowledgement and smiles, carefully avoiding contact with Pepe. Pepe sniffs the air, obviously noting the smell of fresh baking, looks at me expectantly and wags his tail. I automatically reach down to pat his head and he snaps at my fingers, missing me by a couple of centimetres. My mother hoots with laughter.

"That's his little trick. He makes you think he's friendly, then he tries to bite you. He's so funny, don't you think? Clever boy, clever little dog," she says. She reaches down to stroke him and for some reason, he lets her do so without snapping.

"I see you've found your dog," I say. "I thought Papa had a different type of dog in mind. One he could take to work, like a terrier perhaps."

My mother starts to laugh again. "You think I'm having this dog? Why would anyone want this ugly dog? Your Ollee is bad enough, he's an odd-looking bag of bones, but this one is just plain ugly, inside and out."

"But you're walking him. He's in your charge," I say.

"Sometimes I walk with Madame Gambil," she replies, "but I wouldn't want to live with her. I'm simply trying out walking with a dog on a lead to see if I can manage, and at the same time, I'm giving this pathetic creature some exercise. Your daft friend, Sarah, thinks I'll warm to him but I won't. He's snappy, he's bad tempered and he smells a bit strange. He'd be impossible to live with."

Byron and I exchange glances and I know exactly what he's thinking. My mother has perfectly described herself. He turns away, trying to suppress a laugh. I too, am struggling.

"Well I have to go now, Danielle, Monsieur," mother says. "I must return Pepe before the shelter thinks they've got rid of him permanently. Your Papa and I are going to look at a little dog tomorrow. I'll let you know how we get on."

She walks away towards the riverside where the shelter has a single storey building and some land. Pepe continues to snap and snarl and I can hear my mother laughing unkindly whenever he scares someone.

"I'm sorry to say, Danielle, but your mother is an awful woman and she would really enjoy owning that horrible dog. They could both grumble and snap and snarl at people. They'd be company for each other."

I have to agree with Byron. They really do deserve each other.

"Anyway," he says, changing the subject. "What are you up to today? Do you have time to have lunch with me?"

I explain that I'm going out to the Moliner house once again to speak to Jacques.

"Jacques? Why Jacques? He adored Michelle. You'd be much better speaking to that sister of hers, Helene."

"Helene? But she's so sweet. She looks as if she couldn't hurt a fly."

"Maybe so, but remember Michelle stole everything from her when she married Jacques; she ruined Helene's life. It's true that Michelle handed her crumbs from her table, gave her a job and put a roof over her head. But Helene lives in a tiny rented apartment, works like a donkey and had to continually thank her sister for the privilege. It must have been very hard on her day after day, year after year. If you're looking at a crime of passion, then my money is on Helene."

I hadn't considered Helene once I knew she had nothing to gain financially from her sister's death. I still cannot agree that she'd be capable of such a cold-blooded murder. Perhaps I'm wrong. Perhaps none of the people I know are responsible. It surely must be the work of a desperate criminal and that places Guy Legler or Juan Gonzales firmly in the frame.

Chapter 28

The new doormat has *bienvenue* – welcome – emblazoned in bright red on it and that isn't the only thing that's changed. When Jacques opens the door to us he's smiling. The smell of fresh baking and coffee fills the hallway and music fills the house.

"Helene is in the kitchen," he explains as we walk along the corridor to the lounge room. "She's hired Cosette Dupre to work in the agency with Marie and I think it's a much better arrangement. Cosette has twenty years of experience and with Marie's help, she'll soon sort out the business. Marie isn't too happy, she expected to be the manager, but Helene doesn't think she's up to it. It's time for change and Helene knows best."

"I'm sure she does," I agree.

Everything about the house has changed in small, but defining ways. The lounge is no longer stark and minimalist. The sofas now are piled with bright scatter cushions and ornaments adorn the shelves that were once bare. There are family photographs in mismatched frames on the modern sideboard and I notice only one of them contains Michelle. A token picture, I suspect, from when she attended a business dinner. It does nothing to flatter her, as her mouth is scowling in it. I'd been told that this house was designed with Helene's good taste and style, but now it also contains her soul. Little of Michelle remains.

Within a minute of our sitting down on the plush sofa, Helene enters the room, wheeling a trolley carrying delicate little cakes and a pot of coffee.

"You'll have something with us," she says. It's a statement rather than an enquiry. "Jacques and I so much appreciate everything you're doing for us. Don't we, dear?"

Jacques nods in agreement and nibbles on a delicate morsel. "This cake is delicious," he says. "You must try one, Danielle, and you too, Officer," he says to Paul. "Helene is a marvellous cook and baker." He pats his belly. "I'll need to be careful, or I'll be the size of a house," he adds.

Helene beams. "That's one of the reasons I've decided to hand over the management of the office to Cosette, and why I've given up my apartment to move in here," she explains. "This man has no idea how to look after himself. He needs someone to clean and cook and generally run this house."

"So everything is gradually returning to normal," Paul says.

"Better than normal," Jacques replies then he blushes and looks down at his feet, suddenly aware of what he's said.

There is an awkward silence. I clear my throat. "If you'd care to show me the desk, please," I say and I stand up.

"Of course, Danielle, of course, the key is in the room. Follow me please."

I walk behind Helene down the corridor to a small room at the back of the house. All it contains is a large office desk with two, deep drawers on either side of the kneehole and a single office chair. There is a telephone on the desk.

"I've always hated this room," Helene says. "I don't know how Michelle could lock herself away in here for hours at a time. It's so stark and depressing. I'm going to brighten it up and turn it into my sewing room. This house could do with some new soft furnishings. Anyway, I'm rambling on. I'll leave you alone. You'll be able to find your way back to the lounge when you're finished I'm sure, and in the meantime, I'll pour your officer another cup of coffee."

"His name's Paul," I say. "And given the opportunity he'll eat every cake on the plate. Be aware, he's a very greedy young man," I reply.

Helene laughs. I've put her completely at her ease. Good, I think, now for some digging. She seems too cheerful to have so recently lost her sister and in such an appalling way and she has taken over the household role of *maîtresse* very quickly and easily. I'm beginning to wonder if perhaps there has always been something going on between Helene and Jacques. Perhaps Jacques dalliances took place much closer to home than anybody suspected.

It takes me only a few minutes to rifle through the drawers. There is nothing of significance contained in them, but as I try to close the overstuffed, lower, left-hand drawer a stapler sticks it and I reach in to free it. My hand brushes something taped to the underside of the upper drawer and I pull at it to release it. It's an envelope. Michelle's name is written on the outside. Carefully I open the seal and remove the single sheet of paper contained within. The letter is handwritten, it reads *—Sister, I can never forgive you, never, never, ever. You have broken my heart. How could you be so cruel? You don't even love Jacques, you just want his money. Remember I know your sordid secret and I promise you this, if you do not look after me, I'll tell everyone what you did. I'd tell Jacques now if I was as cruel as you, but I don't want to destroy him. I love him too much. If you ever hurt him, I'll kill you. I hate you with every breath I take. When you die, I hope you burn in Hell for eternity.*

I'm stunned. The letter is discoloured with age. The words are so full of hurt and venom. It must have been taped under the drawer for years. Byron's words come flooding back to me – 'If you're looking for a crime of passion, then my money is on Helene,' he said. I carefully place the letter in my pocket. Maybe he's right, I think.

I return to the lounge to collect Paul. "You were quick, Boss," he says, giving me a knowing look. "Find anything?"

"No nothing there I'm afraid," I reply. "We'd better be going, Paul. Thank you for your hospitality," I say to Jacques and Helene.

I'm anxious to get away. I need space to think about what I've found. I should really question Helene about the letter, and more importantly, her feelings about her late sister, but Jacques is obviously involved with her and Jacques is my boss's cousin. What a mess, what an awful mess.

Chapter 29

I feel I have to know more about the Moliner/Lacroix family and who better to ask but the family doctor? Once the lunch break is over, I leave the office and drop in to the practice of Doctor Poullet. Being from one of the original Catalan families in the region, I'm sure this family would consult someone of their own class and stature. If not Poullet, then I'm sure he'd know who else I should ask. When I arrive, Poullet is not at his consulting room and is not due to arrive until late afternoon as he is only seeing two patients today. Daphne, his secretary, telephones his home and he says I can see him there. When I arrive, he shows me into his study.

"This better not be work," he says. "I'm taking a couple of hours off. My wife wants me to arrange a holiday for us and I've been attempting to deal with a budget airline for an hour and a half. If I could pay for a better company I would, but this cheap company are the only ones that fly where my wife wants to go. Typical. All these questions – do you want luggage? I ask you, how stupid! Do they think a man can travel on holiday for a week with one set of clothes? Do you want to book your seat? Am I expected to travel in the pilot's lap or perhaps in the toilet? Of course I want a seat. Insurance, yes or no? Do they expect to crash the plane, lose my luggage or make me ill? If I have to deal with this for much longer, I'll have a stroke and then there will be no need for their insurance. I'll be dead."

"I want to ask you some questions about the Moliner family and especially the sister, Helene Lacroix. How about we do a deal? I'll help you book your holiday, because I'm used to this company as I've flown with them before, and you can answer a couple of questions for me while I confirm your booking."

"Deal," he says. "The paper with the details is next to the keyboard. Do you want a coffee?"

I decline the coffee and before very long, I have made the flight booking for him, arranged a car hire – although heaven help the car hire company; with the way Poullet drives they'd better have insurance – and I've even booked a hotel for the duration of their stay.

"Marvellous, Danielle, I can't thank you enough. If I may ask one favour, please do not tell my wife you did this. Let her think it was I, her clever husband. I don't want her to think I'm feeble-minded and can't even book a holiday. Now, you had some questions?"

Poullet gives me a brief history of the families, mostly what I already knew. However, one thing I did not know was that when Jacques broke up with Helene in favour of Michelle, Helene was admitted to hospital suffering from depression.

"I shouldn't really be disclosing this information," Poullet says. "But, given our friendship and our working relationship, I'll save you the time of going through official channels. I trust you'll be discreet."

"Of course," I reply. "You know I'd never betray our friendship."

"Will you have a Ricard?" he asks, reaching for the bottle on his desk. "I usually indulge at this time of the day."

"I'm not really meant to be drinking alcohol when I'm on duty, but I won't tell if you don't," I reply.

He pours us both a glass of the poison-coloured liquid, adding water from a crystal jug which causes it to turn cloudy-white. "Odd the way it changes," he observes.

"You said Helene was admitted to hospital. Was it serious, did she try to harm herself?"

"She attacked Michelle with a pair of scissors. Michelle's arm was cut as she tried to defend herself. You probably never noticed, but she had a scar on her forearm from the attack. Nobody blamed Helene, she was distraught. Her sister had betrayed her in the cruellest way by stealing her fiancé. The family put Helene in hospital for a month until the whole episode died down."

"But the sisters worked together? Michelle gave Helene a job and paid for her rented apartment. Surely they must have forgiven each other for that to happen."

"Maybe, maybe not," he says guardedly.

"What do you know that you're not telling me, my friend?"

"This is highly confidential, Danielle. Nobody must ever know what I'm about to impart. If it's discovered I've revealed this information, I'll be struck off. Worse, you might have to put your old friend in jail."

He stares hard into my eyes. I sit up in my chair and gulp down some of the *pastis*.

"Michelle became pregnant when she and Jacques were first married. I suspect the baby wasn't his. Helene accompanied Michelle to Spain, where the baby was aborted without Jacques knowledge that she was ever pregnant. I suspect Jacques would have accepted the child as his own flesh and blood. He was desperate for a family, but Michelle wasn't interested. Helene knew that Michelle never wanted children which made it even more difficult for Helene, seeing the man she loved denied the life he should have had with her."

That explains the letter, I think. It must have been written soon after the abortion. That's the sordid secret. That's what gave Helene some limited power over her sister. She couldn't push it too far, or Michelle would have let her tell Jacques because Michelle didn't really care. She seemed to have always done the bare minimum for Helene and Jacques. They were a minor annoyance which she dealt with in the quickest and easiest way. I now know Helene hated her sister with a passion, but would she have taken such drastic action after all these years? Would she have murdered her? What could possibly have driven her over the edge?

I finish my drink, thank Poullet for his time and leave my friend to impress his wife with their holiday. Helene's letter is still in my pocket. Nobody knows it exists, and for the time being, it will remain that way.

Chapter 30

It's before eight o'clock in the morning and my mobile is ringing. Who on earth would telephone this early, I wonder. When I answer, it's Monsieur Claude.

"Danielle, I'm sorry to call so early, but it's an emergency. My life is in danger. I've been threatened."

"Calm down, Claude," I say. He's obviously very upset. "Start at the beginning. Tell me what's happened."

Patricia is sitting at the kitchen table having breakfast and she looks at me while holding her coffee cup suspended in front of her lips.

"What's wrong?" she mouths. I shrug. She sips her coffee but keeps watching me for an answer.

"The Spaniard, Gonzales, he telephoned. He said I took his money. I don't know anything about his money. I never saw any money."

"Okay, Claude, stay calm. When did he telephone?"

"This morning, just a few minutes ago, I am alone at the spa. I was just about to open the offices. Although my secretary was complaining yesterday of someone calling and hanging up as soon as she answered, she thought something was wrong with the phone line, but I think it was him. I think the silent calls were Gonzales, trying to discover if I was here."

"What exactly did he say to you?"

"He said his money must have been in the safe in the studio, because there's nowhere else it could be. He's searched everywhere else and spoken to everyone who could possibly have it. He's convinced that either Patricia or I have his money and he wants it back. I told him the safe was empty when it was opened by the police, but he doesn't believe me."

"How does he know about Patricia being involved with the building?"

"I don't know, but he does, – perhaps Guy Legler told him. I don't know what to do, Danielle. What should I do if he comes here? You'd better warn Patricia."

"Stay calm, Claude, you are not alone in the building as there are people already having treatments at the spa. Don't open the offices until your secretary arrives. You'll see her through the window of the door. I'm going to telephone Laurent and ask him to come and see you. He'll take your statement and alert all the other police offices to look out for Gonzales. We'll soon find him and put an end to his threats."

"I'm scared, Danielle. I'm sure he killed Legler. If he thinks I have his money, he might hurt me. He's a big man, Danielle. I'd be no match for a monster like him."

"I'll find him, Claude. I promise you, I'll find him and when I do, I'll lock him up. He won't harm you."

I wish I could believe what I'm telling him, but I don't. I manage to get him off the phone and I call Laurent and ask him to get straight over to the spa. Then I explain to Patricia what's happened.

"Oh, Danielle, we've had several missed calls with withheld numbers here. There were at least seven yesterday. I was out all day. I'd recognise the numbers if it had been friends or business acquaintances phoning. Do you think he'll come after me? Should we offer him some of the money?"

An icy chill runs down my spine. I really thought we were home and dry. I thought Gonzales had given up and was lying low. He's a dangerous criminal and he might well seek out Patricia.

"We're giving him nothing. That money is ours. Keep the doors locked, Patricia. Don't let anyone in without first looking through the window to see who it is. If you have to go out, call a friend, like Sarah or Marjorie, to drive you and keep Ollee with you at all times. We're going to find this man and put a stop to him. Don't worry, darling, the police will find him and arrest him."

I feel nervous leaving her alone, but I have no choice. When I'm at the office I'll be able to contact Detective Gerard in Perpignan for help. If ever there was a time to pull in a favour, this is it.

Chapter 31

I am frantic with worry. I'm not sure what to do. How can I stop this man when he's not scared off by a murder charge being held over him? I arrive at the office before nine o'clock and Paul arrives at the same time. Quickly, I explain the situation and tell him I'm going to phone Perpignan and I must not be disturbed unless Patricia calls. I'm immediately put through to Detective Gerard.

"Danielle, bonjour," he says. "How nice to hear from you, have you something to report? Any further on with your case?"

I quickly explain the problem with Juan Gonzales and ask Gerard for his help.

"I see, Danielle," he says. "This man hasn't actually threatened Monsieur Claude or your friend Patricia. He hasn't hurt either of them and he's simply wanted for questioning in the Legler case at the moment. Is that correct?"

My hackles are rising. His response is not what I expected. He seems hesitant.

"Detective Gerard," I say through gritted teeth. "You do understand this is directly affecting me and my family. Apart from Guy Legler, who is dead, Juan Gonzales is the only possible suspect in the Moliner case other than your cousin. You know what it's like to have family worries and I do hope you'll pull out all the stops to help me." It's a veiled threat mentioning his cousin, but I feel it's necessary.

"Of course, Danielle, I hope you didn't think I was trying to avoid the issue. Family must always come first, and as you say, this man is likely responsible for Michelle's murder, as well as Legler's. He mistakenly thinks Michelle took his money, but the chances are Legler squirreled it away. I'll put any resources you require into locating Juan Gonzales. Tell me what you need. Once we get him, you'll be able to close the book on both cases."

I'm not exactly sure what help he can give me, so I ask for extra officers and some dedicated administrative assistants to help with the search. He agrees to my request but I can't help thinking there's little he can do. I'm afraid it will be down to me and my team to catch up with this man, and when I do meet up with him, somehow, I'll need to find a way to arrest him or scare him away.

* * *

The next couple of days pass in a blur of fear and worry. There has been no contact from Gonzales, either to Claude or Patricia. I'm relieved when the weekend comes around and I can stay close to my friend.

"I'm meeting your papa at the orchard today," Patricia says. "He telephoned to say he's bringing his new dog. You can drop me and Ollee off there, meet up with your papa and see his dog, then leave us to it. I'm spending some time learning about beekeeping and I know they make you nervous. I'll be perfectly okay with your papa and two dogs. I'll take my mobile and call you when we want a lift home."

She's right, I'd much rather spend my time in the garden and she should be perfectly safe with Papa and the dogs. Patricia packs a picnic for herself and Papa and with Ollee, we climb into the car. The dog has his nose firmly against the basket, sniffing loudly, all the way to the orchard, but at least he's not trying to lick my ear. When we arrive Papa and his dog come to the edge of the field to greet us. Her name is Kiki and Ollee takes to the little, tan and white terrier bitch immediately.

"What a sweet little dog," I say. "So much nicer than the ugly, bad-tempered thing Mama was walking in town."

"Ah, about that," Papa says. "I'm afraid to tell you we still have Pepe. We now have two dogs. Pepe is your Mama's dog. He makes her laugh and Kiki loves him. He's been neutered, so it's not a problem having a male and a female. We won't end up with a litter."

Patricia looks at my face and starts to laugh. Then Papa laughs.

"Your face is a picture of dismay," Patricia announces.

"Pepe makes your Mama very happy," Papa says trying to gain my approval. "She takes him out walking at least twice a day."

"She lets him snap at people. If she's not careful, she might receive a caution from the police," I reply. "Or worse, maybe even a fine."

We chat some more and I'm about to leave when my Papa says, "I nearly forgot girls, there was a man waiting here when I arrived, a huge man, tall and broad, he looked like a weightlifter. He said he wanted to speak to you, Patricia. He said he'd call the house at two o'clock."

Patricia is white faced. "He came here, Danielle," she says.

"I'll deal with this," I say. Don't think about it again. You two enjoy your day. Call when you want a lift home."

Before Patricia can protest, I get into my car and drive off. I'm not sure what I'm going to do about Juan Gonzales, but it had better be good enough to get rid of him permanently.

Chapter 32

I can't settle down so I clock watch as I pace the floor asking myself 'what if'. What if he phones and threatens me? What if he says he'll harm Patricia? What if he arrives at the door instead of telephoning? What if he sets fire to my house? What if he won't take no for an answer? A person can drive themselves mad with what ifs.

The minutes' tick by. I'm fatigued, I feel drained, but still I pace. "Ring," I scream at the phone. "Ring, why don't you? I want this to be over." I pour myself a brandy. "Stay calm," I say to the empty room. "You're no use to anyone if you don't stay calm."

At precisely two o'clock the telephone rings, and I run across the room to answer it.

"Hello," I say. "Who is it?" I'm trying to sound calm, but my stomach is churning and my gut is on fire.

"I want my money," a gruff voice says. "Do you hear me, Patricia? You have my money and I want it."

At the sound of Patricia's name on that criminal's lips, fear leaves me and I'm suddenly cold and angry. I tell him he's talking to a police officer. I tell him I live here with Patricia and she has no idea where his money is. I tell him that when the safe was opened several police officers were in the room and we found nothing. The safe was empty. I urge him to come into the police station and give himself up. He responds with a wry laugh and hangs up.

That could have been a whole lot worse, I think. I feel less afraid now that I've spoken to him. I think I won that round.

The phone rings again and I practically jump out of my skin. My hand is shaking as I lift the receiver to my ear.

"Hello, hello, Danielle, it's Patricia, did he phone? Is everything okay?"

I exhale my bated breath and wipe the sweat from my face with my hand. "Everything's fine, Patricia," I say. "I don't think he'll call again. He knows the police are after him now, so he'll probably head back across the border to Spain. Are you finished at the orchard? Do you want me to collect you now?"

There's a sob in her voice. "I've been worried sick," she says. "If you're sure everything's okay, we'll remain here for about another hour. Can you collect us then?"

"No problem, I'll do that," I reply.

When I hang up the phone I start to shake uncontrollably and for some reason, I burst into tears and sob my heart out.

* * *

My Papa has told Patricia that she needn't do anything with the orchard or the bees even though he won't be around until mid-week. He and my mother have decided to spend a couple of days with their dogs, so they can try to train them and get them used to being a family. They are meeting up with another couple of beekeepers who also have dogs. I'm delighted for them, as I can't remember when they last spent time together socialising.

I'll be on my own tomorrow, as Patricia is taking Ollee to visit her friends Frederick and Anna at their vineyard. I'm driving her there very early in the morning and she plans to stay overnight. Freddy is coming into town on Monday afternoon and he'll bring her back. I could go too – I am invited – but I make an excuse so I can stay close to home, just in case Gonzales tries to get in touch again.

"Will you be all right on your own?" Patricia asks as she steps out of the car at the vineyard on Sunday morning. "You won't be lonely, will you?"

"Don't worry about me," I reply. "If I want company, I'll call Byron. You just enjoy yourself and remember to bring home some of their good wine."

As I drive off, Ollee runs after the car, barking. Clearly, he can't make up his mind which one of us he'd prefer to stay with. I slow the car and he stops in his tracks then turns and runs back to Patricia – I guess she's always going to win.

The weekend passes quickly and by Monday afternoon, everything is back as it should be. Patricia and Ollee are home. Papa phones to give me a progress report on the dogs. He tells me that Pepe has almost stopped biting people, but he still growls at them. A slight improvement, I suppose.

"Mama will be disappointed," I say and he laughs.

The weather has changed. It's cloudy and there's light rain falling, making the office a bit cooler. There are fewer stupid people coming in to ask questions. Weaklings, I think, a little drizzle of rain and they stay indoors.

I'm having a relaxing and pleasant day until I receive a call from Marie's husband Franck to tell us he's discovered a body at my orchard. Then the chaos returns.

Chapter 33

When Paul and I arrive, I see Madame Ancel standing on her side of the perimeter fence that separates her land from mine. A few feet away, in the orchard, Franck is waiting beside the body. Madame Ancel and Franck are speaking to each other over the fence, but their conversation ends abruptly as Paul and I walk towards them. The body is midway between the tool shed and the gate, about ten metres from the road. A top-of-the-range Peugeot 508 RHX is parked at the side of the road. This car would cost me a year's wages, so I know it's not Franck's.

"Bonjour Franck, Madame Ancel," I say. "This must be a bit upsetting for you both." They nod in agreement.

"I was mending the fence when I saw him lying here. There was nothing I could do for him. He was already dead," Franck says.

"Did you touch the body?" I ask.

"Yes, I rolled him over onto his back. I tried to help him, but it was far too late." Franck's eyes are downcast and he shifts uncomfortably from one foot to the other. "Did I do something wrong? Should I have left him face down? I didn't know what to do."

"You did everything you could, Franck," I say, trying to reassure him. "If you would be so kind, Madame Ancel," I say, turning to her. "Some sweet coffee for Franck, please, he's had a shock."

"Yes, Officer, I'll bring a tray. I'll make some for us all," she replies, relieved to have something to do. Madame Ancel walks off towards her house.

"He's a huge man," Paul observes. "It must have taken all your strength, Franck, to roll this big lump over onto his back."

"This is Juan Gonzales," I state. "Half the police forces in the region are searching for him in connection with two murders."

"You'd better call Poullet," I instruct Paul. "Tell him the corpse is in the middle of a field so he's not to wear his best shoes. He'll still moan, but at least he'll be forewarned."

Madame Ancel returns with the coffees and we gulp down the sweet liquid. I ask Madame Ancel and Franck to come into the office at their earliest convenience, to make statements. Then I tell them they may now go home, which they are grateful to do. Poullet arrives half an hour later.

"Another day, another body," he says, trying to be amusing. He's wearing blue hiking boots, a yellow waistcoat over his shirt and he has a battered old hat perched on his head. He cuts a comical figure. With his rotund belly, he reminds me of the children's book character Paddington Bear. With difficulty, Poullet kneels down to inspect the corpse.

"I'm glad I won't have to move this body from the field. They'll need a small crane to shift him," he mutters. "Anaphylactic shock, I suspect. Bee stings on his face and arms, several of them. The stings are still attached to the body. Did you find an EpiPen?"

"You mean this?" Paul asks, holding what seems to be a syringe in his gloved hand.

"Is there no box?" Poullet asks. "Let me see what you have, Paul." He inspects the syringe. "This has been used, but given the amount of bee stings, one pen wouldn't have been enough. For a man this size, he'd have needed two and very quick intervention at the hospital. I bet there are others in his car. You might want to check. A person with this severe form of allergy wouldn't go anywhere without them. I wonder what brought him to this field?"

"My tool shed has been broken into," I state. "The lock's smashed. This man has been searching everywhere for money he said Michelle stole for him. Monsieur Claude and Patricia rented a studio apartment to Michelle. He's been harassing them and everyone else who had any dealings with Michelle. He broke into the studio and killed his brother-in-law Guy Legler, who was also Michelle's lover. He smashed up Pascal Boutiere's office and frightened the poor man half to death. Perhaps he thought something was hidden in the shed."

"He must have been desperate. He must have believed something was indeed hidden there," Poullet says. "Someone who suffers from this type of violent allergic reaction would know the risks of coming into a field containing bee hives. One sting could cause chest wheeze, confusion, falling blood pressure and unconsciousness in minutes, not to mention the swelling of the body which would be most uncomfortable and frightening. Because he's midway between the shed and his car, I think he probably tried to reach another shot of adrenalin, but didn't make it. He was overcome very quickly because of the amount of venom in his system."

"Was his death an accident?" Paul asks.

"Misadventure, I'd say," Poullet replies. "Damned bad luck. Still it saves the court wasting time trying him for murder and saves us taxpayers a large amount of money to pay for the privilege. Help me up, Paul," Poullet says, trying to raise his bulk from the ground. We each give him a hand and pull him to his feet. "You can move the body now," he says. "Better order that crane," he suggests.

"He can talk," Paul mutters as Poullet waddles off. "We could have done with a crane to lift his fat bulk."

Before I get back into my car I telephone Patricia, to tell her that our worries are over. I knew as soon as I saw his huge frame lying in the field, that Juan Gonzales would cause us no more trouble. The relief in Patricia's voice is palpable.

"Thank God, Danielle, thank God. I don't mind telling you, I was really scared, but now I feel so uplifted. I think we should treat ourselves with some of the money, perhaps a holiday, maybe a weekend in Paris. It's definitely ours to keep now," she says.

And maybe I'll buy Papa a few more bee hives, I think. I still dislike the evil little stingers, but I'm prepared to make compromises.

Chapter 34

It's been just over a month since the death of Juan Gonzales and Patricia and I are sitting having breakfast at the kitchen table, looking forward to our trip to Paris next weekend. When we are there, we'll visit an acquaintance of ours who is a celebrity chef. Patricia and I helped him when his mother died tragically and we've kept in touch ever since. Patricia now supplies his restaurant and his delicatessen with pickles and preserves, and this benefits both their businesses. He's promised us a delicious dinner at his award-winning restaurant and I know we won't be disappointed. Papa is going to take care of our animals while we are away, so we have nothing to worry about.

Detective Gerard was delighted when I accepted Juan Gonzales as Michelle's killer, because it cleared his family of any involvement. However, I'm quite sure Helene Lacroix murdered her sister in a fit of rage, and who could blame her? She and Jacques are blissfully happy and are to be quietly married in Spain next month. People will talk, but they'll soon get over it. According to Poullet, they've already sealed the deal, so to speak because Helene is pregnant. She will be an older mother as she is already forty, but this child will be a blessing for them both and will be well loved. I could have investigated further and perhaps even have prised a confession out of Helene, but why bother? Juan Gonzales was guilty of one murder, so why not two? Why destroy the lives of decent people for a bitch like Michelle? It would benefit no-one.

Antonia Gonzales was much more upset over the death of her brother than the killing of her husband, although the blow has been softened by the fact that she'll inherit all his property and money. She can spend her way out of sorrow.

My Papa and mother are often seen out together with their dogs, but whilst Kiki is loved and greeted by everyone, Pepe continues to snap and snarl, much to the amusement of my mother. She is rather a strange woman and I still don't fully trust her to be pleasant to me, but time and age have mellowed her a bit and maybe with luck, they will mellow her dog as well.

Patricia and I are chatting about this and that and we're planning our day when she becomes rather serious and says, "It was quite shocking the way Juan Gonzales died, don't you think? Who would have thought a simple bee sting could kill a big man like him?"

I stare into her sparkling blue eyes. Even though this awful man terrorised her, she still feels for him and is upset by the unusual way in which he died.

"Patricia, darling," I say. "I've something I want to tell you. It's been bothering me for weeks. I don't want to upset you, but I'd like to get it off my chest. It concerns the death of Juan Gonzales."

She tops up our coffees and waits patiently for me to speak. Her expression is serious.

"I was terrified when Gonzales phoned," I begin. "He wouldn't give up. He said he would hurt you if I didn't find his money and he gave me forty-eight hours to get back to him."

Her hand covers her mouth, she is clearly shocked.

"I knew he was allergic to bees, because his sister told me when I called on her. I saw his EpiPens on her coffee table and I asked her about them. That's when I knew what I had to do. It was my only choice. I decided to scare him off. I wanted him to think I had the upper hand and was unafraid.

I asked him to meet me at the orchard on Sunday at eleven o'clock, knowing I'd be back from delivering you to Frederick and Anna's house by ten-thirty. I told Gonzales his money was hidden at the orchard and that neither you nor Claude knew anything about it. You and Papa would both be away, so neither of you could be involved. Franck mentioned to me that he was going to mend the perimeter fence on the Monday. It's Madame Ancel's fence, so she will pay, but he needed our permission to work from our land. I knew Gonzales's body was lying close to the fence so I simply waited for Franck to find it."

"Oh, Danielle, you took a terrible risk! Gonzales might have killed you." Patricia's eyes are full of tears.

"Don't be upset, darling," I say. "I had a plan, a good plan and it worked. It worked too well and unfortunately, Gonzales was killed."

We both sip our coffees then I continue.

"When I arrived at the orchard, I put on Papa's bee suit and veil, then I hid behind the shed and waited. At precisely eleven o'clock, Gonzales arrived. He made straight for the shed and banged on the door. I stepped out from behind it and surprised him. He laughed when he saw me dressed in the suit and veil. He laughed at me until he realised just how near we were to the beehives, then a look of fear passed over his face.

"Where's my money?" he said. "Give me my money and you'll never hear from me again."

Gonzales began to walk towards me and I quickly stepped behind one of the hives. When he was only a short distance away I banged on the hive with my gloved hand and the bees began to fly about angrily. Gonzales was terrified. He began to swat at them with his hands, and inevitably he was stung. He began to panic and so did I. He took an EpiPen from his trouser pocket and he was struggling to remove the cap, but by then he'd been stung numerous times and his fingers were already swollen and clumsy.

"Let me help you," I said, but before I could reach him his chest was wheezing and he'd collapsed to his knees. He was dead within minutes. I wasn't sorry he was dead, but the circumstances were shocking. I'd inadvertently caused him to die. You must believe me, darling, I only intended to frighten him off."

"How awful for you, Danielle, how terrible it must have been to witness such a ghastly death. Why didn't you tell me about this sooner? You know you can tell me anything."

She reaches out to take my hands in hers and squeezes them reassuringly.

"It's all over now. You must put all thoughts of that criminal out of your mind. We have a holiday to look forward to and we'll never mention his name again, but we will enjoy his money," she adds with a cheeky smile. "We deserve to have it, after all you've been through."

Now I've unburdened myself I feel totally relaxed. Dear Patricia, I can always rely on her to put things into perspective.

I look out of the window and see the sun is shining brightly and there are no clouds in the sky. It's going to be another hot day. The temperature is rising. It makes me think that perhaps this year we should hire Franck to build us a swimming pool. We both enjoy swimming and we can certainly afford it.

Chapter 35

ANOTHER TRUTH

What is the truth and is it always wise to tell? Do you tell your friend that her boyfriend is weak and her baby is ugly? Or do you tell her that he's a prince and her child is a cherub? Do you tell your boss that you detest his stupidity and you should really have his job because you're smarter than him? Or do you agree with all he says because you don't want to be victimised or fired? You know what I'm saying my friend, don't you? We all have to make decisions to lie or not to lie. That is indeed the question.

I told Detective Gerard the truth he wanted to hear. The only truth he would accept, but I have his card marked and he knows it. I have the bullet of truth firmly held in my grasp to fire anytime I see fit. I'm angry that he was prepared to see me drown without throwing out his hand to save me. He didn't care that my darling Patricia was in danger, it wasn't his problem and he was prepared to do nothing until it reached its inevitable end, whatever that might have been. I know Helene Lacroix murdered her sister. After years of putting up with Michelle's appalling treatment, the incident over the paella pan must have been the last straw. It's strange how we can often put up with quite major transgressions, yet something relatively trivial can push us over the edge. I'm certain Gerard's cousin Jacques also knows. How could he not? But as I said before, I'll keep that truth safe and sound for now. Besides, Michelle deserved to die.

Then there is the truth I told Patricia about Juan Gonzales's death. She felt sorry for me witnessing such a death and it was terrible. But what I told her wasn't the whole truth, it was just the part she needed to hear.

When Gonzales threatened to harm Patricia, my fear turned to anger. I was white cold with rage. I had to stop him at any cost. I did lure him to the orchard and I was wearing my Papa's bee suit and veil, that part is true. He did arrive at exactly eleven o'clock as I knew he would, because he was a stickler for time. When he arrived, I was not hiding behind the shed, I was inside and it was unlocked. Later, I would break the lock to support my story. When Gonzales opened the door, he was faced with me holding a gun. Apart from the purpose of cleaning it, my gun has never been out of its holster and I sincerely hoped I wouldn't have to use it. Although given that Gonzales was wanted for two murders and looking at the difference in our sizes, if attacked by him, I would have been justified. He was scared, really scared, he tried to reason with me, even begged me to be sensible and let him walk away, but I couldn't. I wouldn't.

I forced him to back away from me. He was watching the gun so carefully, he didn't realise his back was against a beehive until he bumped into it. The look of horror on his face when he realised what he'd done was a picture I'll never forget. He was stung almost immediately and in his panic, he slapped at the angry creatures and they stung and they stung until his chest was wheezing and he sank to his knees. Still, he managed to reach into his trouser pocket and take out his EpiPen, but he didn't have the strength to stop me taking it from him grasp and discharging it against his leather shoe instead of his thigh. The funny thing was, he thought, when I took it, I was going to use it to save him. Imagine that? As if I would. Instead, I threw the discharged syringe to the ground and walked away before anyone saw me. I knew he would die quickly and I expected Franck would discover him when he arrived to mend the perimeter fence. Gentle, dependable Franck didn't let me down.

Now my friend, you know the whole truth. I would call it justice, wouldn't you?

End

A Message from Danielle

Thank you for reading 'Deadly Degrees in the Pyrenees,' I do hope you enjoyed it. If you've read the first four books in the 'Death in the Pyrenees' series, you will know the journey I've travelled to reach this stage and what a journey it has been. However, if you've had no previous knowledge of my life and would and would like to catch up with my ups and downs and highs and lows, you can meet my friends and colleagues and some of the less desirable individuals who have lived and died here - available now the first four books.

Till soon
Danielle

Other books by Elly Grant

Palm Trees in the Pyrenees
Take one rookie female cop
Add a dash or two of mysterious death
And a heap of prejudice and suspicion
Place all in a small French spa town
And stir well
Turn up the heat
And simmer until thoroughly cooked
The result will be surprising

Palm Trees in the Pyrenees is the first book in the series 'Death in the Pyrenees.' It gives you an insight into the workings and atmosphere of small town France against a background of gender, sexual, racial and religious prejudice.

The story unfolds, told by Danielle a single, downtrodden, thirty-year-old, who is the only cop in the small Pyrenean town. She feels unappreciated and unnoticed, having been passed over for promotion in favour of her male colleagues working in the region. But everything is about to change. The sudden and mysterious death of a much hated, locally-based Englishman will have far reaching affects.

sample - Chapter 1

His death occurred quickly and almost silently. It took only seconds of tumbling and clawing at air before the inevitable thud as he hit the ground. He landed in the space in front of the bedroom window of the basement apartment. As no-one was home at the time and, as the flat was below ground level, he may have gone unnoticed but for the insistent yapping of the scrawny, aged poodle belonging to the equally scrawny and aged Madame Laurent.

Indeed, everything in the town continued as normal for a few moments. The husbands who'd been sent to collect the baguettes for breakfast had stopped, as usual, at the bar to enjoy a customary glass of pastis and a chat with the patron and other customers. Women gathered in the little square beside the river, where the daily produce market took place, to haggle for fruit, vegetables and honey before moving the queue to the *boucherie* to choose the meat for their evening meals.

Yes, that day began like any other. It was a cold, crisp, February morning and the sky was a bright, clear blue just as it had been every morning since the start of the year. The yellow Mimosa shone out luminously in the morning sunshine from the dark green of the Pyrenees.

Gradually, word filtered out of the *boucherie* and down the line of waiting women that the first spring lamb of the season had made its way onto the butcher's counter and everyone wanted some. Conversation switched from whether Madame Portes actually grew the Brussels sprouts she sold on her stall, or simply bought them at the supermarket in Perpignan then resold them at a higher price; to speculating whether or not there would be sufficient lamb to go around. A notable panic rippled down the queue at the very thought of there not being enough, as none of the women wanted to disappoint her family. That would be unacceptable in this small Pyrenean spa town, as in this small town, like many others in the region, a woman's place as housewife and mother was esteemed and revered. Even though many held jobs outside the home, their responsibility to their family was paramount.

Yes, everyone followed their usual routine until the siren blared out – twice. The siren was a wartime relic that had never been decommissioned, even though the war had ended over half a century before. It was retained as a means of summoning the *pompiers*, who were not only the local firemen but also paramedics. One blast of the siren was used when there was a minor road accident or if someone took unwell at the spa, but two blasts was for something extremely serious.

The last time there were two blasts was when a very drunken Jean-Claude accidentally shot Monsieur Reynard while mistaking him for a boar. Fortunately, Monsieur Reynard recovered, but he still had a piece of shot lodged in his head which caused his eye to squint when he was tired. This served as a constant reminder to Jean-Claude of what he'd done as he had to see Monsieur Reynard every day in the cherry orchard where they both worked.

On hearing two blasts of the siren everyone stopped in their tracks and everything seemed to stand still. A hush fell over the town as people strained to listen for the shrill sounds of the approaching emergency vehicles. Some craned their necks skyward hoping to see the police helicopter arrive from Perpignan, and whilst all were shocked that something serious had occurred, they were also thrilled by the prospect of exciting, breaking news. Gradually, the chattering restarted. Shopping was forgotten and the market abandoned. The *boucherie* was left unattended as its patron followed the crowd of women making their way to the main street. In the bar the glasses of pastis were hastily swallowed instead of being leisurely sipped as everyone rushed to see what had happened.

As well as police and *pompiers*, a large and rather confused group of onlookers arrived outside an apartment building owned by an English couple called Carter. They arrived on foot and on bicycles. They brought ageing relatives, pre-school children, prams and shopping. Some even brought their dogs. Everyone peered and stared and chatted to each other. It was like a party without the balloons or streamers.

There was a buzz of nervous excitement as the police from the neighbouring larger town began to cordon off the area around the apartment block with tape. Monsieur Brune was told in no uncertain terms to restrain his dog, as it kept running over to where the body lay, and was contaminating the area in more ways than one.

A slim woman wearing a crumpled linen dress was sitting on a chair in the paved garden of the apartment block, just inside the police line. Her elbows rested on her knees and she held her head in her hands. Her limp, brown hair hung over her face. Every so often she lifted her chin, opened her eyes and took in great, gasping breaths of air as if she was in danger of suffocating. Her whole body shook. Madame Carter – Belinda – hadn't actually fainted, but she was close to it. Her skin was clammy and her pallor grey. Her eyes threatened at any moment to roll back in their sockets and blot out the horror of what she'd just seen.

She was being supported by her husband, David, who was visibly shocked. His tall frame sagged as if his thin legs could no longer support his weight and he kept swiping away tears from his face with the backs of his hands. He looked dazed, and from time to time, he covered his mouth with his hand as if trying to hold in his emotions but he was completely overcome.

The noise from the crowd became louder and more excitable and words like 'accident', 'suicide' and even 'murder' abounded. Claudette, the owner of the bar that stood across the street from the incident, supplied the chair on which Belinda now sat. She realized that she was in a very privileged position, being inside the police line, so Claudette stayed close to the chair and Belinda. She patted the back of Belinda's hand distractedly, while endeavouring to overhear tasty morsels of conversation to pass on to her rapt audience. The day was turning into a circus and everyone wanted to be part of the show.

Finally, a specialist team arrived. There were detectives, uniformed officers, secretaries, people who dealt with forensics and even a dog handler. The tiny police office was not big enough to hold them all so they commandeered a room at the *Mairie*, which is our town hall.

It took the detectives three days to take statements and talk to the people who were present in the building when the man, named Steven Gold, fell. Three days of eating in local restaurants and drinking in the bars much to the delight of the proprietors. I presumed these privileged few had expense accounts, a facility we local police did not enjoy. I assumed that my hard-earned taxes paid for these expense accounts, yet none of my so called colleagues asked me to join them.

They were constantly being accosted by members of the public and pumped for information. Indeed, everyone in the town wanted to be their friend and be a party to a secret they could pass on to someone else. There was a buzz of excitement about the place that I hadn't experienced for a very long time. People who hadn't attended church for years suddenly wanted to speak to the priest. The doctor who'd attended the corpse had a full appointment book. And everyone wanted to buy me a drink so they could ask me questions. I thought it would never end. But it did. As quickly as it had started, everybody packed up, and then they were gone.

Grass Grows in the Pyrenees
Take one female cop and
Add a dash of power
Throw in a dangerous gangster
Some violent men
And a whole bunch of cannabis
Sprinkle around a small French spa town
And mix thoroughly
Cook on a hot grill until the truth is revealed

Grass Grows in the Pyrenees, second book in the series "Death in the Pyrenees," gives an insight into the workings and atmosphere of a small French town and the surrounding mountains, in the Eastern Pyrenees.

The story unfolds told by Danielle, a single, thirty-year-old, recently promoted cop. The sudden and mysterious death of a local farmer suspected of growing cannabis, opens a 'Pandora's' box of trouble. It's a race against time to stop the gangsters before the town, and everyone in it, is damaged beyond repair.

sample - Chapter 1

For a moment, he flew horizontally as if launched like a paper aeroplane from the mountain top then an elegant swan dive carried him over the craggy stone face of the mountainside. There was no thrashing of limbs or clawing at air, he fell silently and gracefully until a sickening crack echoed through the valley as bone and flesh crunched and crumpled on a rocky outcrop. The impact bounced him into the air and flipped him in a perfect somersault, knocking the shoes from his feet. Then he continued his descent until he came into contact with the grassy slope near the bottom of the mountain, where he skidded and rolled before coming to a halt against a rock.

His body lay on its back in an untidy heap with arms and legs and shoulders and hips smashed and broken. The bones stuck out at impossible angles and blood pooled around him. He lay like that for almost three days. During that time the vultures had a feast. There are several species of these birds in the mountains of the Pyrenees and all had their fill of him. Rodents and insects had also taken their toll on the body and, by the time he was discovered, he was unrecognisable.

A hunter found him while walking with his dog and, although he was used to seeing death, the sight of this man's ravaged face, with black holes where his eyes should have been, made him vomit.

Jean-Luc still wore the suit that he'd carefully dressed in for his meeting three days before. It looked incongruous on him in his present condition and in these surroundings. His wallet was still in his pocket and his wedding ring was still on his finger, nothing had been stolen.

The alarm had been raised by his business partner when he failed to turn up for their meeting but of course no one had searched for him in this place. This valley was outside of town and on the other side of the mountain from where he'd lived. He wasn't meant to be anywhere near to this place.

His wife hadn't been overly concerned when he didn't return because he often went on drinking binges with his cronies and he'd disappeared for several days on other occasions. She was just pleased if he eventually came home sober because he had a foul temper and he was a very nasty drunk. Indeed, she knew how to make herself scarce when he was drunk, as more often than not, she would feel the impact of a well-aimed punch or a kick. Drunk or sober he lashed out with deadly accuracy and he was quick on his feet.

When he was finally discovered all the emergency services were called into action. The *pompiers*, who were firemen and trained paramedics, the police and the doctor, all arrived at the scene and an ambulance was summoned to remove the body to the morgue.

Everyone assumed he'd died as a result of his rapid descent from the mountain top and the subsequent impact on the ground below. But what they all wanted to know was whether his death was a tragic accident, or suicide, or perhaps something darker and more sinister, and why was he in this place so far from his home or from town? Many questions had to be answered and, being the most senior police officer in this area, meant that I was the person who'd be asking the questions.

Red Light in the Pyrenees
Take one respected female cop
Add two or three drops of violent death
Some ladies of the night
And a bucket full of blood
Place all in, and around, a small French spa town
Stir constantly with money and greed
Until all becomes clear
The result will be very satisfying

Red light in the Pyrenees, third in the series Death in the Pyrenees, gives you an insight into the workings and atmosphere of a small French town in the Eastern Pyrenees. The story unfolds, told by Danielle, a single, thirty-something, female cop. The sudden and violent death of a local Madam brings fear to her working girls and unsettles the town. But doesn't every cloud have a silver lining? Danielle follows the twists and turns of events until a surprising truth is revealed. Hold your breath, it's a bumpy ride.

sample – Chapter 1

The body of Madame Henriette is lying through the broken window of the kitchen door with the lower part of the frame supporting her lifeless corpse. Her head, shoulder and one arm hang outside, while the rest of her remains inside, as if she has endeavoured to fly, Superman style, through the window and become stuck. She is slumped, slightly bent at the knees, but with both feet still touching the floor. Her body is surrounded by jagged shards of broken glass.

From the kitchen this is all one sees. It is not until you open the window to the side of the door and look through it, that you see the blood. Indeed quite a large area of the tiny courtyard has been spattered with gore as Madame Henriette's life has pumped out of her. One shard has sliced through her throat and by the amount of blood around, it seems to have severed her jugular. She must have been rendered unconscious almost immediately as she has made no effort to lift herself off the dagger-like pieces of glass which are sticking out from the frame.

There is blood on the pot plants and on the flowering creeper which grows up the wall, dividing this house from the neighbour's. It has also sprayed the small, hand crafted, wrought iron table and chairs. The blood is beginning to turn black in the morning sun and there's a sizeable puddle congealing on the ground under the body. This will need to be spread with sawdust when the clean up begins, I think to myself.

There is rather a lot of blood on Madame Henriette's head as it has run down her face from the gaping wound on her throat, but it's still possible to see that her hair is well-styled and her face is fully made up. Her clothes are tight and rather too sexy for a woman of her age and her push-up bra and fish-net stockings seem inappropriate at this time of the morning. If you didn't know any better, you would assume that Madame Henriette is simply a lady of growing years trying desperately to hold on to her youth, but to her neighbours and those of us who have had dealings with her, the truth is much less forgiving. Madame Henriette is indeed a Madame. She is a lady of the night, a peddler of prostitutes, and this building which she owns is a brothel.

The house of Madame Henriette is situated in the old part of town where the cobbled streets are so narrow that only one car may pass at a time. All the buildings are tall and slim and made of stone. Each is distinguished from the next by different coloured shutters and different degrees of weathering to the facade.

When entering this house one would pass through a small door which is cut in a much larger, heavier one. The magnificent carved entrance looks overdressed in this street and harks back to a time when this area was much grander. Nowadays everyone wants modern and the town has spread out with alarming speed from this central point. The wealthy live in the suburbs. They have gardens, swimming pools and pizza ovens. From once being uptown and chic, these streets have become dreary and they now contain a lower class of citizen. They are a melting pot of students, foreigners and people who survive on state benefits. Sometimes holidaymakers rent here thinking the area is quaint and having the desire to experience a 'typical' French house in a 'typical' French street.

After entering through the door, which is immediately off the road, you would find yourself in a narrow hallway with a magnificent, old and ornate, tiled floor. A curved stone stairway with an iron banister rail then takes you to the upper floors. On the first floor, if you turned to your right, you would find yourself in the sitting room where Madame Henriette offered her guests some wine as they waited for one of her 'nieces' to fetch them. Then they would be taken to one of the bedrooms which are situated on the upper floors. To the left is the kitchen but few meals were cooked there. Food was usually very quickly thrown together from a selection of cold meats, cheese and bread, then hastily eaten by the girls as they grabbed a few spare moments between clients. All, of course, was washed down with glasses of heavy, red, cheap, local wine. The wine made both the food and the clients more palatable.

The body of Madame Henriette was discovered by her maid Eva who is a rather scrawny girl aged about twenty. She has mousy brown hair and grubby looking skin peppered with acne scars. Every day Eva came to work for Madame, her duties being to wash the sheets, clean the house and bring in the food from the market. She was also responsible for buying condoms and checking that each bedroom had a plentiful supply. Madame Henriette was fastidious about health and safety and would never allow sexual contact without condoms.

On discovering the body of her mistress, the shocked young woman fled the house and ran screaming into the street. One of the neighbours heard the screams and chose, on this occasion, not to ignore the noises coming from the vicinity of the house but instead telephoned for the emergency services and this is where my story begins.

Dead End in the Pyrenees
Take a highly-respected female cop
Add a bunch of greedy people
And place all in a small French town
Throw in a large helping of opportunity, lies and deceit
Add a pinch in prejudice
A twist of resentment
And dot with death and despair.
Be prepared for some shocking revelations
Dangerous predators are everywhere
Then sit down, relax and enjoy
With a dash or two of humour
And plenty of curiosity

Dead End in the Pyrenees' is the fourth book in Elly Grant's 'Death in the Pyrenees' series. Follow Danielle, a female cop located in a small town on the French side of the Pyrenees as she tries to solve a murder at the local spa. This story is about life in a small French town, local events, colourful characters, prejudice and of course death.

sample – Chapter 1

The blow to his head wasn't hard enough to render Monsieur Dupont unconscious, but it stupefied him. Blood poured profusely from a deep scalp wound down into his left eye. He flopped onto the recently-washed tiles at the side of the Roman bath then floundered at the edge, frantically trying to stop his body from slipping completely into the pool. His upper torso overhung the edge, his hands slapping at the water as he tried to right himself. He was aware of the metal chair, which was attached to a hoist to enable the disabled to enter the water, beginning to descend. As it lowered it trapped Monsieur Dupont, forcing his head and shoulders under the water. He struggled, his toes drumming the moist tiles, his arms making a flapping motion, but he was hopelessly stuck. Soon he succumbed. Brimstone-smelling steam rose from the surface of the spa pool and silence returned.

When Madame Georges arrived for work she was surprised to hear a low, electronic, whirring sound coming from the pool area. She couldn't think what it was. Surely the machinery and gadgets, designed to treat all manner of ailments, had been switched off at the close of business the night before? The last treatments were usually completed by 7pm, then everyone went home leaving Monsieur Dupont, the caretaker, to lock up.

Following the sound, Madame Georges entered the majestic Roman spa. The double doors swung silently closed behind her as she made her way towards the pool. She was aware of her feet, still encased in outdoor shoes, making a slapping sound on the tiled floor. Madame Georges immediately noticed that the hoist chair was down and something was bundled up beneath it at the water's edge, but as her spectacles were steamed-up from the damp atmosphere, she couldn't tell what that something was until she was practically on top of it.

"Oh, *mon Dieu*," she said aloud, on realising that what had looked like a bundle of rags, was in fact, a man.

A wave of shock passed through her body, she took off her glasses with shaking hands, cleaned them on the hem of her blouse then stared again. It was definitely a man. His body was still and there was what seemed to be blood, gathered in a puddle on the tiles beneath it. Madame Georges did not immediately recognise the person, as the head and shoulders were under water. All the staff at 'les thermes' wore pink track-suits and trainers to work, and the guests were usually attired in white towelling, dressing gowns and blue rubber pool shoes. This person was clothed in a dark-coloured suit and had formal shoes on his feet.

Regaining some of her composure, Madame Georges turned and ran back through the double swing doors towards the office. She used her key to let herself in then immediately pressed the button to sound the alarm. The alarm was a wartime relic, a former air-raid siren, still used to alert people to an emergency. It wailed out over the valley and across the mountains twice. People who would normally have gone back to sleep at the first blast were now fully awake. The queue of chattering shoppers, waiting in line at the *boulangerie* to buy their baguettes, fell silent, each person straining to listen for approaching emergency vehicles. This double call was used only for the most serious of incidents.

Madame Georges sank into a chair and picked up the phone and dialled the emergency number to report what she'd discovered.

"Oh, *mon Dieu, mon Dieu*, a man is dead! I'm sure he is dead! There has been an accident, I think. Assistance, *s'il vous plait*, please come at once, please help me, I am alone here," she said, when her call was answered. Madame Georges had seen death before many times. The spa attracted the sick and the old searching for cures for various ailments and many of them spent the last days of their lives there, but this was different.

Like a well-oiled machine, everything flowed into action. Before very long the *pompiers*, who are firemen and trained paramedics arrived, along with an ambulance and a local practitioner named Doctor Poullet. A crowd began to gather in the street outside. But prior to this whole circus kicking off, I was the first on the scene accompanied by one of my trainee officers. We managed to calm down Madame Georges before securing the area and this is where my story begins.

The Unravelling of Thomas Malone

The mutilated corpse of a young prostitute is discovered in a squalid apartment.

Angela Murphy has recently started working as a detective on the mean streets of Glasgow. Just days into the job she's called to attend this grisly murder. She is shocked by the horror of the scene. It's a ghastly sight of blood and despair.

To her boss, Frank Martin, there's something horribly familiar about the scene.

Is this the work of a copycat killer?

Will he strike again?

With limited resources and practically no experience, Angela is desperate to prove herself.

But is her enthusiasm sufficient?

Can she succeed before the killer strikes again?

and here's the first few pages to sample -

Prologue

Thomas Malone remembered very clearly the first time he heard the voice. He was twelve years, five months and three days old. He knew that for a fact because it was January 15th, the same day his mother died.

Thomas lived with his mother Clare in the south side of Glasgow. Their home was a main door apartment in a Victorian terrace. The area had never been grand, but in its time, it housed many incomers to the city. First the Irish, then Jews escaping from Eastern Europe, Italians, Polish, Greeks, Pakistanis, they'd all lived there and built communities. Many of these families became the backbone of Glasgow society. However, situations changed and governments came and went and now the same terraces were the dumping ground for economic migrants who had no intention of working legally, but sought an easy existence within the soft welfare state system.

A large number of the properties were in the hands of unscrupulous landlords who were only interested in making money. They didn't care who they housed as long as the rent was paid. So as well as the people fleeing the system, there were also the vulnerable who they exploited. Drug addicts, alcoholics, prostitutes, young single mothers with no support, they were easy pickings for the gangsters. The whole area and the people living within it smacked of decay. It had become a no-go district for decent folk, but to Thomas Malone, it was simply home.

Thomas and his mother moved to their apartment on Westmoreland Street when Clare fell out with her parents. The truth was they really didn't want their wayward daughter living with them anymore. They were embarrassed by her friends and hated their drinking and loud music. When Clare became pregnant, it was the last straw. Thomas's grandparents were honest, hard-working, middle-class people who had two other children living at home to consider. So when Clare stormed out one day after yet another row with her mother, they let her go. She waited in a hostel for homeless women for three weeks, before she realised they weren't coming to fetch her home and that's when Clare finally grew up and took charge of her life in the only way she knew how.

When Thomas walked home from school along Westmoreland Street, he didn't see that the building's façades were weather worn and blackened with grime from traffic fumes. To outsiders they looked shabby and were reminiscent of a mouth full of rotting teeth, but to Thomas they were familiar and comforting. He didn't notice the litter strewn on the road, the odd discarded shoe, rags snagged on railings, or graffiti declaring 'Joe's a wanker' or 'Mags a slag'. He functioned, each day like the one before, never asking for anything because there was never any money to spare.

He was used to the many 'uncles' who visited his mother. Some were kind to him and gave him money to go to the cinema, but many were drunken and violent. Thomas knew to keep away from them. Sometimes he slept on the stairs in the close rather than in his bed so he could avoid any conflict. He kept a blanket and a cushion in a cardboard box by the door for such occasions. Many a time, when he returned from school, he found his mother with her face battered and bruised, crying because the latest 'uncle' had left, never to return. It was far from being an ideal life, but it was all he knew so he had no other expectations.

It was a very cold day, and as he hurried home from school, Thomas's breath froze in great puffs in front of him. He was a skinny boy, small for his age with pixie features common to children of alcoholics. His school shirt and thin blazer did little to keep him warm and he rubbed his bare hands together in an attempt to stop them from hurting. He was glad his school bag was a rucksack because he could sling it over his shoulder to protect his back from the icy wind. As his home drew near his fast walk became a jog, then a run, his lungs were sore from inhaling the cold air, but he didn't care, he would soon be indoors. He would soon be able to open and heat a tin of soup for his dinner and it would fill him up and warm him through. He hoped his mother had remembered to buy some bread to dunk.

As Thomas approached the front door something didn't seem right, he could see that it was slightly ajar and the door was usually kept locked. There was a shoe shaped imprint on the front step, it was red and sticky and Thomas thought it might be blood. There was a red smear on the cream paint of the door frame, which he was sure was blood. Thomas pushed the door and it opened with a creak; there were more bloody prints in the hallway.

Thomas took in a great breath and held it as he made his way down the hall towards the kitchen. He could hear the radio playing softly. Someone was singing 'When I fall in love'. He could smell his mother's perfume – it was strong as if the whole bottle had been spilled. The kitchen looked like a bomb had hit it. His mother wasn't much of a housekeeper and the house was usually untidy, but not like this. There was broken crockery and glassware everywhere and the radio, which was plugged in, was hanging by its wire from the socket on the wall, dangling down in front of the kitchen base unit. A large knife was sticking up from the table where it was embedded in the wood. The floor was sticky with blood, a great pool of it spread from the sink to the door, and in the middle of the pool lay the body of Thomas's mother. She was on her side with one arm outstretched, as if she were trying to reach for the door. Her lips were twisted into a grimace, her eyes were wide open and her throat was sliced with a jagged cut from ear-to-ear. Clare's long brown hair was stuck to her head and to the floor with blood and her cotton housecoat was parted slightly to expose one, blood-smeared breast.

Thomas felt his skinny legs give from under him; he sank to his knees and his mother's blood smeared his trousers and shoes. He could hear a terrible sound filling the room, a guttural, animal keening which reached a crescendo in a shrieking howl. Over and over the noise came, filling his ears and his mind with terror. Then he heard the voice in his head.

"It's all right, Son," it said. "Everything will be all right. I'm with you now and I'll help you."

He felt strong arms lift him from the floor and a policeman wrapped him in a blanket.

"Don't be frightened," the voice told him. "Just go with the policeman. Someone else will sort out this mess. It's not your problem. Forget about it."

"Thank you," he mouthed, but no sound came out.

The policeman gathered Thomas in his arms and carried him from the room. It was the last time he ever saw his mother and he cannot remember now how she looked before she was murdered. The voice in his head, the voice that helped him then, remains with him today guiding and instructing him; often bullying, it rules his every thought. Sometimes, Thomas gets angry with it, but he always obeys it.

The Coming of the Lord

Breaking the Thomas Malone case was an achievement but nothing could prepare DC Angela Murphy or her colleagues for the challenge ahead.

Escaped psychopathic sociopath John Baptiste is big, powerful and totally out of control. Guided by his perverse religious interpretation of morality, he wreaks havoc.

An under-resourced police department struggles to cope, not only with this new threat, but also the ruthless antics of ganglord, Jackie McGeachy.

Pressure mounts along with the body count.

Glasgow has never felt more dangerous.

Never Ever Leave Me

'Never Ever Leave Me' is a modern christmas romance

Katy Bradley had a perfect life, or so she thought. Perfect husband, perfect job and a perfect home until one day, one awful day when everything fell apart.

Full of fear and dread, Katy had no choice but to run, but would her split-second decision carry her forward to safety or back to the depths of despair? A chance encounter with a handsome stranger gives her hope.

Never ever leave me, sees Katy trapped between two worlds, her future and her past. Will she have the strength to survive? Will she ever find happiness again?

Death at Presley Park
In the center of a leafy suburb, everyone is having fun until the unthinkable happens. The man walks into the middle of the picnic ground seemingly unnoticed and without warning, opens fire indiscriminately into the startled crowd. People collapse, wounded, and dying. Those who can, flee for their lives.

Who is this madman and why is he here? And when stakes are high, who will become a hero and who will abandon their friends?

Elly Grant's 'Death At Presley Park' is a convincing psychological thriller.

But Billy Can't Fly
At over six feet tall, blonde and blue-eyed, Billy looks like an Adonis, but he is simple minded, not the full shilling, one slice less than a sandwich, not quite right in the head. When you meet him, you might not notice at first, but after a couple of minutes it becomes apparent. The lights are on but nobody's home. In Billy's mind, he's Superman, a righter of wrongs, a saver of souls and that's where it all goes wrong. He interacts with the people he meets at a bus stop; Jez, a rich public schoolboy; Melanie, the office slut; Bella Worthington, the leader of the local W.I. and David, a gay, Jewish teacher. This book moves along quickly as each character tells their part of the tale. Billy's story is darkly funny, poignant, and tragic. Full of stereotypical prejudices, it offends on every level, but is difficult to put down.

Released by Elly Grant Together with Zach Abrams

Twists and Turns
With fear, horror, death and despair, these stories will surprise you, scare you and occasionally make you smile. *Twists and Turns* offer the reader thought provoking tales. Whether you have a minute to spare or an hour or more, open *Twists and Turns* for a world full of mystery, murder, revenge and intrigue. A unique collaboration from the authors Elly Grant and Zach Abrams

Here's the index of Twists and Turns -
Table of Contents
A selection of stories by Elly Grant and Zach Abrams ranging in length across flash fiction (under 250 words), short (under 1000 words) medium (under 5000 words) and long (approx. 16,000 words)

- Trials and Tribulations (medium) by Elly Grant
- Runswick Bay (medium) by Elly Grant
- Alice (short) by Elly Grant
- Hide and Seek (flash) by Zach Abrams
- Snip, Snip (medium) by Zach Abrams
- Come See what I Dug Up in the Sand, Daddy (short) by Elly Grant
- Room Mate (flash) by Zach Abrams
- Courting Disaster (medium) by Zach Abrams
- Crash (flash) by Zach Abrams
- Submarine (medium) by Elly Grant
- Dilemma (flash) by Zach Abrams
- Grass is Greener (medium) by Zach Abrams
- Missing (flash) by Elly Grant
- Time to Kill (medium) by Elly Grant
- Fight (flash) by Zach Abrams
- Just Desserts (medium) by Elly Grant
- Interruption (flash) by Zach Abrams
- I've Got Your Number (medium) by Elly Grant
- Rhetoric (flash) by Zach Abrams
- Keep It to Yourself (medium) by Zach Abrams

- Lost, Never to be Found] (medium) by Zach Abrams
- Man of Principal] (flash) by Zach Abrams
- Witness After the Fact] (medium) by Zach Abrams
- Overheated] (flash) by Zach Abrams
- Wedded Blitz] (medium) by Elly Grant
- Taken Care] (flash) by Zach Abrams
- The Others] (short) by Elly Grant
- Waiting for Martha] (long) by Elly Grant

and here's the first few pages to sample -

Waiting for Martha

The 'whoooo aaaaah' accompanied by blood curdling shrieks sent the Campbell brothers screaming down the path. They tore along the street without a backward glance. Martha Davis and her three companions doubled up with laughter. They were all dressed as zombies and, to the naïve eyes of primary school-aged children, they were the real thing.

"Did you see the middle one move?" Alan Edwards asked. "He could be a candidate for the Olympics. He easily left his big brother behind."

"That's because the older one's a lard ass," John Collins replied unkindly. "His bum cheeks wobbled like a jelly. Fat kids shouldn't wear lycra. If the real Superman was that chunky he'd never get off the ground."

"The middle one overtook him because he was trying to help the younger one and was holding his hand," Martha observed. "I'm sure that little fellow pee-ed his pants, he was terrified. He's only about five."

"Yeah, great, isn't it?" Fiona Bell added laughing. "I love Halloween, don't you?" she said clapping her gloved hands together with pleasure.

The teenagers had hidden around the corner of Alan's house to jump out at unsuspecting children who came trick or treating. They were all aged fifteen except for John Collins whose birthday had been in June, he was sixteen but looked older. He was a big lad, tall and broad with an athletic build, he looked like a grown-up where the others still looked like children. Fiona Bell was nearly sixteen her birthday was on the fifth of November, Guy Fawkes night, so the group would be celebrating next week with fireworks. She was the spitting image of her mother being of medium height with long blonde hair and a heart shaped pretty face. Alan Edwards's birthday was in January. He was short with straggly black hair and he was a bit of a joker. Martha Davis, the baby of the group, was born in March and was a willowy looking beauty with Titian coloured hair. They were in the same class at school and had a reputation for being cool and edgy. None of them was ever actually caught for their various misdemeanours, but they were often seen running away from trouble. Being teenagers they thought they knew it all and, smoking, drinking, wearing only black and never telling their parents anything, was par for the course. Living in a village meant they didn't have easy access to drugs but the friends made roll-ups using everything from dried orange peel to crushed tree bark and convinced each other it had some psychedelic effect. They'd all been born in the village and had been friends since playgroup. They trusted one another with their worries and secrets and their friendships endured through petty squabbles and jealousies. Although unrelated, they were like a family.

By seven o'clock the procession of 'victims' had all but dried up – the word had got out, it seemed – so Martha and her friends decided to change venue.

"Time to go to church," Alan suggested. "If we hide just inside the gates of the churchyard, we'll get them as they walk by."

"That's a great idea," John added. "They'll think we've risen out of one of the churchyard graves. We'll scare the shit out of the little darlings."

"You lot go ahead and I'll catch you up. I'm going home for a warmer sweater and a quick bite to eat. I've not had my dinner yet and I'm starving. I'll just be about half an hour," Martha assured.

"Why didn't you grab something to eat before you came out? The rest of us did. Now you'll miss out on some of the fun," Fiona said, sounding disappointed. Martha was her best girl friend and she didn't want to be stuck on her own with the two boys. They could get incredibly silly without Martha. She was the mother figure of the group and she always managed to stop them from going too far.

"Don't worry Fiona, I'll not be long, and you two," she said pointing to the boys, "Behave yourselves."

"Yes Mom," they replied in unison, hanging their heads and pulling comical faces.

"See what I have to put up with when you're not there, anyone would think they were two years old."

Martha stared at her three friends, her face had a serious expression and for a moment it looked as if she might cry. "I love you guys," she said. "I'll be as quick as I can."

"Are you okay?" Fiona asked. "You look a bit upset."

"I'm fine, really fine. My eyes are just watering with the cold. It's freezing out here."

Martha gave each of them a hug and off she raced towards her home. The others quickly made their way to the church and positioned themselves behind one of the large wrought iron gates. The gates hadn't been closed for over fifty years and ivy grew thickly round them affording the teenagers cover. For the next forty minutes, they had a ball scaring adults and children alike until one of their teachers, Mr. Johnston, came along. As the three friends jumped out shrieking, he clutched his heart and fell to the ground. They thought they'd killed him. They were kneeling on the ground beside him each trying to decide how to do CPR when he suddenly sat up and shouted "Got ya!" The tables were well and truly turned and they nearly jumped out of their skins.

"It's not so funny when you're on the receiving end, is it?" he said rising to his feet. "Haven't you got homes to go to? And where's the fourth one? Where's your friend, Martha?"

"She went home for some food," Fiona said. "She should have been back by now."

"I think you should all run along and find her. You've done enough damage here for one night."

Mr. Johnston brushed himself down and walked away. After their shock, the three friends had indeed had enough.

"Martha should have been here ages ago," Alan said. "I'm getting cold now. Let's go to her house and see what's keeping her."

"Good idea," John agreed.

"But what if she's on her way and we miss her?" Fiona protested.

"Come on," Alan said, pulling her arm. "I'm not waiting any longer and you can't stay here on your own. A real zombie might leap out of a grave and get you. If Martha arrives and we're gone, she'll go home and she'll find us there."

"I suppose you're right," Fiona conceded.

"I'm always right," Alan said smugly. "Come on, let's get going before my ears fall off with the cold."

The three friends headed along the street towards Martha's home. They were damp and tired and they hoped that Helen Davis, Martha's mum, had hot soup for them. She always had soup on the stove in winter and she fed the three of them as if they were her family.

"I hope Mrs. Davis has pumpkin soup, it's my favourite," John said,

"Yeah, the chilli she puts in it really gives it a kick," Alan agreed.

"Aren't either of you just a teensie bit worried about Martha? She's been gone for over an hour now and she's never usually late," Fiona said. "Get a move on you two, I want to make sure she's all right."

When they reached Martha's house and rang the bell they were surprised when her Dad, Michael, answered instead of her.

"Well, well, what have we here?" he asked, laughing at their attire. "Is Martha hiding? Where is she?"

"She left us over an hour ago, to come home for some food," Fiona said. "We thought she was still here. When did she leave the house?"

"Martha hasn't been home," her father replied. "If this is some sort of Halloween joke, it's not funny." He stared at the teenagers. "The jokes over – where's Martha?"

A chill ran through each of the friends and Fiona's eyes welled with tears. "We don't know," she said helplessly. "If she didn't come home then she's been gone for over an hour. Something might have happened to her, maybe she's fallen. We'd better go back and look for her."

"Wait for me. I'm coming with you," Mr. Davis replied. "I'll just go and tell Martha's Mum what's happening."

After a couple of minutes Michael Davis returned and Helen was with him. When she saw the state Fiona was in, Helen put her arm around the crying girl's shoulders and tried to reassure her, "Don't worry, pet, we'll find her," she said. "She won't have gone far. She probably stopped to chat to someone and lost track of the time."

"We'll split into three groups," Michael Davis said. "Alan and John, you take the street leading to the church. Helen and Fiona, you walk towards the primary school and I'll take the road that goes around the outside of the village. We'll meet back here in half an hour. No, better make it forty-five minutes," he said looking at his watch.

The boys looked uncomfortably at Fiona, they would have much rather stayed together but they had no choice. Mr. Davis had taken control, and as he was an adult and a teacher, they felt they should do what he said. Besides, the sooner they found Martha the sooner they could go home.

They searched the whole village knocking on several doors as they went. The group met up after the arranged forty-five minutes then searched again. By ten o'clock, there was nowhere left to look for her. The next day was a school day and the three teenagers had now reached their curfew, but they were reluctant to go home with Martha still missing. Michael Davis was grim faced. Helen was beginning to panic.

About the Author

Hi, my name is Elly Grant and I like to kill people. I use a variety of methods. Some I drop from a great height, others I drown, but I've nothing against suffocation, poisoning or simply battering a person to death. As long as it grabs my reader's attention, I'm satisfied.

I've written several novels and short stories. My first novel, 'Palm Trees in the Pyrenees' is set in a small town in France. It is published by Author Way Limited. Author Way has already published the next three novels in the series, 'Grass Grows in the Pyrenees,' 'Red Light in the Pyrenees' and 'Dead End in the Pyrenees' as well as a collaboration of short stories called 'Twists and Turns'.

As I live in a small French town in the Eastern Pyrenees, I get inspiration from the way of life and the colourful characters I come across. I don't have to search very hard to find things to write about and living in the most prolific wine producing region in France makes the task so much more delightful.

When I first arrived in this region I was lulled by the gentle pace of life, the friendliness of the people and the simple charm of the place. But dig below the surface and, like people and places the world over, the truth begins to emerge. Petty squabbles, prejudice, jealousy and greed are all there waiting to be discovered. Oh, and what joy in that discovery. So, as I sit in a café, or stroll by the riverside, or walk high into the mountains in the sunshine I greet everyone I meet with a smile and a 'Bonjour' and, being a friendly place, they return the greeting. I people watch as I sip my wine or when I go to buy my baguette. I discover quirkiness and quaintness around every corner. I try to imagine whether the subjects of my scrutiny are nice or nasty and, once I've decided, some of those unsuspecting people, a very select few, I kill.

Perhaps you will visit my town one day. Perhaps you will sit near me in a café or return my smile as I walk past you in the street. Perhaps you will hold my interest for a while, and maybe, just maybe, you will be my next victim. But don't concern yourself too much, because, at least for the time being, I always manage to confine my murderous ways to paper.

Read books from the 'Death in the Pyrenees' series, enter my small French town and meet some of the people who live there – and die there.

To contact the author email to ellygrant@authorway.net

To purchase books by Elly Grant link to http://author.to/ellygrant